VIRAGO
MODERN CLASSICS
585

Beryl Bainbridge

Beryl Bainbridge (1932–2010) wrote eighteen novels, four works of non-fiction and five plays for stage and television. *A Weekend with Claude* was her first published novel. Five of her novels were shortlisted for the Booker Prize; *Every Man for Himself* and *Injury Time* won the Whitbread Prize; *The Bottle Factory Outing* won the Guardian Fiction Prize; and *Master Georgie* won the James Tait Black Memorial Prize. Four of her novels, including *An Awfully Big Adventure*, were adapted for film. In 2011, Bainbridge was honoured posthumously with a special Best of Beryl Man Booker Prize in recognition of her outstanding career. Her final novel, *The Girl in the Polka-dot Dress*, was published in 2011.

By Beryl Bainbridge

NOVELS

A Weekend with Claude
Another Part of the Wood
Harriet Said . . .
The Dressmaker
The Bottle Factory Outing
Sweet William
A Quiet Life
Injury Time
Young Adolf
Winter Garden
Watson's Apology
Filthy Lucre
An Awfully Big Adventure
The Birthday Boys
Every Man for Himself
Master Georgie
According to Queeney
The Girl in the Polka-dot Dress

SHORT STORY COLLECTIONS

Mum and Mr Armitage
Collected Stories

NON-FICTION

English Journey, or the Road to Milton Keynes
Forever England: North and South
Something Happened Yesterday
Front Row: Evenings at the Theatre

A WEEKEND WITH CLAUDE

Beryl Bainbridge

Introduced by Linda Grant

virago

VIRAGO

First published in Great Britain in 1967 by Hutchinson
Revised edition published in 1981 by Gerald Duckworth & Co.
This paperback edition published in 2012 by Virago Press

A CIP catalogue record for this book
is available from the British Library.

ISBN 978-1-84408-854-6

Typeset in Goudy by M Rules
Printed and bound in Great Britain by
Clays Ltd, St Ives plc

Papers used by Virago are from well-managed forests
and other responsible sources.

MIX
Paper from
responsible sources
FSC® C104740

Virago Press
An imprint of
Little, Brown Book Group
100 Victoria Embankment
London EC4Y 0DY

An Hachette UK Company
www.hachette.co.uk

www.virago.co.uk

INTRODUCTION

I first met Beryl Bainbridge not at a literary party but in a minibus en route to Essex in 2002. Also present were her great friend Bernice Rubens, the biographer Michael Holroyd and our publisher Richard Beswick. We were driving to a day for library members to meet authors. At lunch, Beryl ate a few salad leaves and drank a third of a bottle of Scotch, which did not appear to impair her in any way. I was perfectly well aware that I was in the presence of greatness. She was a novelist of a generation before mine, whom I had been reading since my early twenties. She had burst out of some territory where the English middle classes seldom went, and her books had nothing to do with sociology. There was a black heart to them, in a comic chest.

On our return, as we sat in the minibus in the car park waiting for the engine to start, Bernice announced that she was looking forward to getting home and having a cup of tea, which Beryl responded to by shouting, 'What a boring thing to say.' Beryl then turned to Michael and asked, 'Any nice soaps on tonight?' Anxious to make a contribution and a good impression, I pointed out that it was Saturday so it was *Brookside* day.

Everyone brightened. The conversation turned to *EastEnders*, Kat Moon and sexual abuse; Michael confessed he had shed a tear the previous week. We all agreed that we liked soaps. We drove back into London; Beryl had no idea where she was but seemed delighted by all of it. 'Look at the lovely fruit and vegetables,' she cried as we drove down Turnpike Lane.

Beryl and I both grew up in Liverpool, both of us were subject to the then-fashionable elocution lessons intended to free us from what were seen as the career limitations of our accents. But her Liverpool was specific to her imagination: she remade it in her own image. Bainbridge fans divide into those who prefer the later historical novels and the ones who, like me, believe the earlier books were where she revealed her genius. I was sorry when she turned to real people, but she said herself in later life that she had run out of her own experience to write about.

The chronology of her early work is a little confusing. *Harriet Said . . .* was the first novel she wrote and submitted for publication, but it was rejected and did not appear until 1972. Her first published novel, *A Weekend with Claude*, which appeared in 1967, was later substantially revised and reissued in 1981, so this new edition is not the one which its first readers saw. Neither of these are apprentice works, there was nothing for her to be embarrassed about; she was a fully formed writer from the start.

Harriet Said . . . is set just after the war in a Liverpool suburb near the Formby sand dunes where Bainbridge grew up – an unknown part of England, rarely visited, on the outskirts of the port city. Two girls of around thirteen years old make their way to the beach during the school holidays where they become friends with a group of lonely, disappointed middle-aged men. The degree of freedom the two girls are allowed is unimaginable today, but reflects the day-to-day life of the war when enemies were not strangers but aerial bombers, parents were focused on the war effort on the home front and children were expected to be self-reliant.

From the first chapter, we understand that there has been 'an incident'. The territory of sexual abuse of children has been worked so hard in fiction and memoir for the past decade or so that it is startling to see such an early novel which undermines what has come to seem a genre. The story turns out to be considerably more complicated than the usual kiddy fiddlers in the guise of uncles scenario. The unnamed narrator's friend is a girl who is knowing, clever and manipulative and with the chilling disdain and ignorance of youth for the complexities of adult life. The men are targeted, even groomed by the girls: 'We took to going for long walks over the shore, looking for people who by their chosen solitariness must have something to hide.'

Bainbridge understood the minds of young girls in the confusion of puberty, but she also understood, through acute observation, the men whose marriages, jobs, homes have led them to the beach, to look out to sea with hope, longing and despair, their backs against the land. Part of what they have lost is their own youth, life has slipped past under bowler hats and heads rested against antimacassars. They are lost and lonely, the girls encourage conversation. Harriet's friend wants to be admired by Mr Biggs, whom they call the Tsar.

The girls have a hunch that there is something in it for them, but they are not sure what it is. Perhaps it is just a desire for transgression; they are flirtatious and innocent at the same time. Harriet's friend is the weaker party, she appears merely to obey Harriet's instructions, but she leads one of the men on to destruction. When the novel was first offered for publication one editor found the characters too repulsive for fiction. Nearly half a century later, they still shock because of their subversion.

On the last page of *A Weekend with Claude*, a photograph is described in which a group of people are posed, two on the ground, a third scowling on a wrought-iron bench and a fourth, 'isolated, hunched . . . not looking into the camera. The sun had gone behind a cloud. The three friends posed on, marooned in a summer garden.' Photographs like this, of strangers, incite tremendous curiosity. They freeze time in the moment before or just after a row, or a failed pass, or an opened letter imparting news. Even if we are in the pictures ourselves, we examine them and can no longer remember why one person is not smiling, or looking away, the faces seen only by the eye behind the camera.

Two people have come to buy a desk from Claude, an antiques dealer. They notice a photograph and a letter pushed into the back of a drawer, which Claude reclaims. He tells them a brief version of the story of the people in the picture, which is intercut with first-person accounts of the same events by Lily, Victorian Norman and Shebah. These very disparate characters in both age and background have come together for the weekend. Lily, who thinks she is pregnant by a boyfriend who has abandoned her, is determined to sleep with Edward and fool him into thinking he is the father of her baby.

Victorian Norman, so nicknamed because of the high collars he affects, is a working-class autodidact Communist. Lily has inherited a run-down house in Liverpool in which several of the characters seem to have lodged. She has, according to Victorian Norman, 'left home very early, in a stampede of open revolt, splintering in the process the whole framework of her background, so that now she is sad to find there is nothing to return to but ruins'.

Shebah is a sixty-year-old former actress, tiny, Jewish, resentful and paranoid, filled with fantasies of her own persecution, in exile from her community: 'one of those people who once seen are never forgotten. She wears bright red lipstick and her upper lip is quite hairy. Most people refuse to walk down the street with her.'

Apart from Claude, the characters move in a tight orbit around each other, intent on their own minute sensations, grievances and plots for their advancement. It is a claustrophobic novel set in a year, 1960, when the Sixties was still a date, not an era half-buried under social commentary. The poverty of the post-war years, of unfit houses filled with Victorian furniture, bathrooms before showers, sex before contraception, is a bleak dream-like glimpse into life on the undocumented margins.

On the novel's republication, the *Sunday Times* described Bainbridge's genius as lying in 'the comic evocation of the flat and mundane life in which her characters are in perpetual and ineffectual revolt'. The weekenders at Claude's might end up as the hopeless cases on the Formby shore thirty years later, tormented by juvenile girls in Spice Girls T-shirts. Beryl Bainbridge was original in detecting what was unusual in the ordinary and overlooked. She did not think like anyone else; perhaps her early years as an actress gave her a heightened sense of the dramatic, but she kept it under control by writing within a limited dimension. There was always comedy in those margins.

The last time I saw her was at the Booker Prize dinner in 2009. I did not know she was ill. She would struggle to complete her final novel, *The Girl in the Polka-dot Dress*, and she died a year later. Rereading these early novels, I realise that she was a

For my editor, Anna Haycraft

him in a circle laughing at his jokes. Behind the laughter they were afraid of him, as well as envious.

On the other side of the house was the girls' boarding school where Lily, his friend, had gone as a child, long before he had met her. He had bought the house and moved in before he realised that she had gone to school there. Sometimes at night he would lie awake and think how strange it was that Lily had walked in crocodile in the Elizabethan gardens beyond his barn. When Sarah had left him he had telephoned Lily every night and sometimes two or three times during the day just to talk to someone, just so as not to be so alone in the house with the rooms strewn with toys and the cradle empty in the bedroom. He wanted Lily to come and visit him, but she lived up north and she had her own problems; all she could do was hold the telephone two hundred miles away and listen to him talking. She kept telling him that it would be all right, that in time it would stop hurting, that from somewhere someone was coming to him, just like one of those songs she was always humming, 'Some Day my Prince will Come', though God knows it was Lily who needed to believe that, not he. He kept telling her that it wasn't love he wanted – not that ever again – but amnesia. Then Julia had come and tidied away the toys and put the cradle in the loft, hidden his cigarettes and nursed him back to health. Without Julia there would be no house, no barn and no business.

Claude looked across the stone courtyard to the open door of the house and saw Julia pass quickly in red slippers, going into the kitchen to prepare lunch. Against the wall, pressed close to the dried stem of the wistaria, was his youngest son's pram. It was a big pram, an expensive pram, with the edge of a white pillow showing at the hood. He remembered that his other sons had slept out their milky days in a second-hand pram bought for seven-and-six in Camden Town. A thrifty woman, Sarah, in many ways. Bending her golden head, heavy under its weight of hair, she had laid their children one by one in the cheap carriage on the soiled pillow and gone, melon-hipped and honey-mouthed, away from him into their house. Always away from him.

Behind, in the barn, the woman was whispering, and Claude heard the man say, 'Yes, but it's just what we visualised', and he moved his head, because he didn't care at that moment to know what it was other people visualised. He slid his hand into the opening of his check shirt and caressed his breast, massaging the skin for comfort and from habit. He didn't turn round or withdraw his hand when the man said, just behind him, 'My wife and I have decided to take the desk.'

The wife was opening drawers and rummaging inside them. Her fingers searched in the narrow darkness and found something. 'Oh look!' she cried, feeling the evidence first and then seeing it. 'A photograph and a letter.' She held them up in her greedy fingers and waved them about in the air.

'Ah,' said Claude, 'yes, I'm afraid I put them there and forgot, only a few weeks ago.' He moved regretfully towards her. Her scarlet mouth was open in disappointment, her face misted with powder. 'So sorry, my dear,' he said. 'It's nothing more historical than a letter written to me by a friend. It's not much of a find. If you'll look at the date you'll see it was written in 1960. You know, in all my years in the antique business I've yet to come across anything of real significance.'

The woman stood there, holding the letter and the snapshot out of his reach, not wanting to give them up. Claude would have liked to snatch the letter from her, to flick her meanly across the bridge of her tilted nose – there where the powder grains lay like pollen on her skin. They stared at each other.

'We really should be going,' said the husband.

The woman's arm came down at last. She pouted.

'Come across to the house and have some coffee,' said Claude, folding the letter and putting it and the photograph in his pocket. Without waiting for a reply, he led the way out of the barn and across the yard, his hand pinned like a brooch to his heart.

Julia had been peeling potatoes and preparing the child's nappies for washing. Because of the thoroughness with which she did everything, most ordinary household tasks took her far longer than was necessary. The nappies had been soaking all night and were now half-washed, before being boiled and washed yet again. They lay modestly in a blue polythene bucket by the sink and emitted no smell at all.

'Coffee,' said Claude, not unkindly, though he knew this would delay Julia even further and would make her irritable later in the day. 'You are naughty, Claude,' she would scold. 'I've so much to do and you know how I hate getting behind my schedule.'

'What a charming kitchen,' said the woman. She peered with exaggerated interest at two china heads, two rustic sweethearts, cheek to apple cheek, attached to the whitewashed wall. 'Oh how sweet! Aren't they sweet?' As she looked she kicked the polythene bucket, and a small slap of cold water spilled on to her foot. 'Goodness,' she cried and stood there while Claude knelt at her feet and patted her shoe with a dishcloth.

Kneeling as he was, Claude felt the photograph in his pocket stiff against his skin, and beneath his skin his heart beating – beating rather rapidly with the effort of stooping.

It didn't seem so long ago since he had been young, or younger, since he had been two stones lighter, since his wife had left. She had walked so deliberately out of the door, without even a coat; and he had followed her down the street to the bridge and then stopped and watched her walk away from him over the river, her hands by her sides. She had moved out of his life without looking back, without bothering to wave. He had been so ill for a year after her departure over the bridge, out of his reach, that he hadn't been aware of his gradual accumulation of flesh; it had been a surprise for him to find himself at last so large and bulky. Julia thought it was the drink. Probably it was, but privately he believed it was the body's way of protecting itself against being beautiful ever again. There was a time, after all, to cease being beautiful and a time to cease being young, and for him it had been when his wife left him. If he had been less weak he might have been able to keep the children which, like her coat, she had forgotten to take with her, but he had gone into hospital and finally she had fetched them.

Julia began to boil water for the coffee. 'Only Nescaff, I'm afraid,' she said and paused, watching Claude as if half expecting him to say it wouldn't do. But he was busy opening a box which stood on the kitchen table, packed full of china he had collected earlier that morning.

The man who had bought the desk was left standing in the doorway. He had the feeling that if he spoke he wouldn't get a reply, but he couldn't keep silent. 'Anything very interesting, old man?' he said, and added quickly, to fill the void in which Claude went on unwrapping plates: 'Shall I make out a cheque for the desk now, Mr Perkins?'

Claude had rolled up the sleeves of his shirt. His arms were square and hairless, elbow-deep in newspapers. 'Yes, if you like.' At the corner of his mouth he had sucked in a tendril of beard.

There was no room to write on the table, and the only other

surface, the draining board, was wet with soapy water. The man was forced to hold his cheque book high against the wall. He found his eyes level with the two china heads, with the two rosy mouths. As he half-turned to look at his wife, his hand slipped and the book fell to the floor beside the polythene bucket. The half-completed signature blurred. 'Damn,' he said, bending to retrieve the book and flapping it about in the air.

'It's quite all right,' said Claude. 'Don't bother to write another.'

He didn't look up, and the cheque with its tear-stained signature lay on the table among the newspapers.

Outside in the yard the baby woke and began to make small sounds of distress.

'Claude darling, do get him,' said Julia.

'Look at these,' he said. 'Aren't they nice?' He held up one of the plates for Julia's inspection.

'Yes, they are nice.' Head down, her spectacles misty from the steam of the coffee now in the cups, Julia put the sugar bowl on the table amid the papers, and a tin of biscuits.

'Do sit down,' said Claude to the woman. He gathered up quantities of newspaper and dropped them on the kitchen floor. The cheque went too. The man saw it float under the table and come to rest against the leg of a chair.

'I bought these plates from a woman in the next village,' said Claude. 'I constantly buy for money objects that people no longer value. When I was younger I could hardly bear to part with anything I bought. Now I'm not so foolish.'

'I suppose you've hung on to a few things,' the man said, thrusting his fist into the pocket of his trousers. It was a damn fine desk and a damn fine house, but he didn't know how to take this fellow. He couldn't explain it, but the blighter seemed aggressive. And yet it had been he who had suggested they stay for coffee.

'No,' said Claude. 'I haven't. When my wife left me, she didn't even take a toothbrush. But later, when I was ill, she sent a van and cleared me out, lock, stock and barrel.'

The woman sat quite still on her stool at the table.

Julia went out of the kitchen into the yard in her red slippers. The baby's crying suddenly stopped.

Presently she came back into the passage, and they heard her talking to the baby. 'My little lamb, my little honey love, Mummy's little honey cake,' she crooned. She climbed the stairs, and a door closed and clipped short the sweet words.

'Have you ever thought, man,' said Claude, though he was looking at the woman, 'how eatable are the words of endearment, how full of sugar? There's a good reason for it, of course.'

'Oh, what's that?' In spite of himself, the man put the question. He sat down at the table opposite his wife and stirred his coffee.

'Simple,' said Claude. 'The body needs sugar – it's the energy source. At birth a child undergoes six hours of hunger – sometimes more, but six hours is the maximum before the body experiences actual starvation.'

'Really,' said the woman. She had never had children. She had tried, but had failed.

'It's a fact,' said Claude. 'Then the child starts crying – crying because it's starving – and the mother takes over, either with the breast or a bottle.'

The man felt uneasy at the use of the word 'breast'. He had a terrifying image of himself laid against his mother's huge purple nipple. Saliva gathered in his mouth. He glanced at the tailored front of his wife's costume and was aware of Claude saying:

'A child that's denied food when it cries is also denied love, I reckon. The withholding of food by the mother object is a withholding of love. And it doesn't just stop there. Most mentally disturbed adults crave sugar – you know, sweets and sugary drinks, all the fattening things.' He crumpled a piece of newspaper between his fingers and rolled it into a ball. 'They've done some interesting experiments in America. They put three mental patients into a room with two doctors, who gave them the usual shock treatment to the mid-brain. Then they put all sorts of candies and sweets in front of the poor devils and watched them eat. Suddenly they removed all the food and the first patient screamed "For God's sake, give us more love", and the second said to the doctor "Please, Mother" and held out his hands.' Claude opened his own hands in illustration, and the ball of newspaper dropped to the floor.

'But what about the third man,' asked the woman. 'The third patient? What did he say?'

'I really don't remember, my dear.'

'Do you really believe in all this neurotic nonsense?' The man shook his head, as if to clear away doubts. He was surprised at the irritation in his own voice. There was something about this fellow Perkins that made you feel he was being personally vindictive. And he'd damn well let his own child cry long enough out there in the garden – if it *was* his child.

'Certainly I do,' said Claude. 'There's a great deal in it. Otherwise, why should you feel such resentment? We all suffer from the same sense of loss.'

The man couldn't think of a suitable reply. Sweat accumulated under the armpits of his newly laundered striped shirt.

'That's why you girls like having your breasts sucked,' said Claude. 'You know instinctively you're giving the man both food and love.' He leaned forward and put his arm round the woman's shoulders and shook her. 'It's true, isn't it, girl? It's the truth, isn't it?'

She was consumed with embarrassment and excitement. It was as if he had shown her a pack of obscene photographs. His head was so close to hers that the curling strands of his beard touched her cheek. Her husband's face appeared blurred in the little room, and his mouth was open. On his hand he wore a ring his father had given him, a gold ring with a dull green stone. She kept her eyes focused on it, because she felt that if she looked away the link between them would be broken and she would make some wanton remark to this bearded man with his arm so protectively about her shoulders.

'It's been most interesting,' said her husband, frowning. 'But it's time we were moving. It certainly is time.' He stood up and shook himself more securely into the jacket of his grey suit and heard the loose change jingle in his pocket. He was at once wholly himself and solid again. The man was probably round the bend, he thought. Clearly he had an obsession with women's chests.

Julia came back, bringing with her a smell of talcum powder. She was no longer pale or downcast; her lips and cheeks seemed to have filled out and gathered colour from the child.

'I'm sorry to have been so long,' she said, though she knew that her absence had probably been scarcely noticed. She made an affected gesture with her long fingers. 'The baby, you know.'

'They've bought the desk, the one I picked up in Leeds,' said Claude, rising from the table. He lifted the pile of newly acquired plates and carried them to the sink.

'Oh, how nice.' Julia bent and began collecting newspapers from the floor.

'My wife had a bit of a disappointment, though,' said the man, watching his cheque being swept up with the rest of the debris. 'She found a letter and a photograph in the desk, but they belonged to Mr Perkins.'

'I did think it was at least an old will or a treasure map,' complained the woman.

Claude was putting detergent into the bowl in the sink and running hot water. 'Instead of which,' he said through the steam, 'it was merely an old letter of Lily's and a photograph I took in the garden that weekend in the summer.'

'Oh, that one,' said Julia. 'Where is it?'

'In my top pocket.'

Julia drew out the photograph and looked at it. 'It seems such a long time ago,' she said. 'Poor dear Shebah.' She laid it down on the table.

The man stared at the photograph, at the two figures seated on the ground, a man and a girl. Behind them on a bench was an old woman with a bandage round her leg, and a man one seat away. It wasn't a very good photograph, but he pointed at the face of the girl and said, 'Who's that?', half-thinking it might be the missing wife gone with all the furniture – and small blame to her, by the sound of it.

'It's a friend of Claude's, someone very dear to him,' Julia said. 'He's known her for years, haven't you, Claude?'

'Yes,' he said. 'For years.'

Which was the truth. For years and years he had known Lily. He and Sarah had had two rooms and three children when he had first met her. She had lived up at the Heath end of Parliament Hill and they had lived at the bottom. Sometimes she had baby-sat for them, once she had cut Sarah's hair. She had told him about the student she was in love with, back home in Liverpool, who wasn't in love with her. In the secure position of one who already knew the pain of unrequited love, he had advised her to forget him. 'But I can't,' she told him. 'It hurts.' Her next sweetheart, an hotel waiter, had proved no more adequate at loving her in the way she desired, and she had felt hurt again. She leapt from one piece of suffering to another. She insisted that Claude meet all her lovers, because he might be able to persuade them to love her properly. 'You,' she had said, 'are my best friend. You'll know how to put my case.' He hadn't cared for the student, or for the waiter, or for the half-dozen suitors who followed after. He had cared for Billie least of all. Edward, the much-needed Edward, she had brought to him four summers ago, along with her comrade Victorian Norman and her friend Shebah.

He looked down at the plates in the sink and lapped water over the painted flowers. Behind him the man picked up the photograph, scrutinising again the blurred features of the girl. It was as if he held the camera, as if he were about to click the shutter out there in that time past. The lens of his eye blinked and recorded her image, her dark mouth, her white cheeks, her slightly smiling eyes looking straight into his . . .

down, I don't seem to have grown used to having come so far from my childhood environment. Even living in London seems odd, not to mention having a flat with carpets. And my friends are a bit funny. Not exactly funny – not in the ha-ha sense – though I suppose Shebah *is* a bit comical. She's not talking at the moment, which makes her look different, almost clumsy. Just now she sits on a white cane chair, pouting, eyes closed behind her glasses. She likes sitting in the open air among the daisies. Like me, she's probably thinking how they approach most closely to the image she has of herself – little and pretty and white.

I don't really think I'm like a daisy – it's more that I've trained my mind to think these thoughts – and I've found lately that maybe I haven't an image at all. Or if I have, it's blurred. Coming here on the bus I had an image of myself as a chatterer, with 'Oh, that's a lovely house' and 'Oh, what a super house'. At least I said all that because Victorian Norman never said a word, just stared out of the window, and I did want us to sound as if we were animated. Shebah kept handing us sweeties, but I didn't take one. I don't eat sweets any more. Edward sat in front of me, and it meant I could lean forward and put my hand on his neck, and I liked that, because I thought if anyone was watching us it looked as if we had been married for years and I was still adored. I mean, I feel fairly certain I'm still adored – but then I've only known Edward a little while and he doesn't know me very well. I met him at a party, and I always make an impact at first meeting – that is, if the person involved is lost enough, or odd enough, or something. At least it's always been like that before. They usually go off me equally quickly. Edward seems to be the exception at the moment, and he just might marry me if I'm nice enough long enough. And I simply have to get married this time, because of the baby not yet born, and that's why we all came here this weekend – for me to make Edward the father of the baby. I've never been so cunning before. Never. It's not really such a mean trick to play on anyone – well, not on Edward, because he's always smiling at children and patting them on the head. I made Shebah and Norman come with me because they're my friends, and they've spent most of the weekend having little chats with Edward and putting me in a good light. They haven't told me yet what they said, but it must have been nice, and maybe tomorrow Edward will ask me to marry him. With a bit of an effort I could be a good wife. I could even help him in his career. I don't know much about geology – I haven't had time to go to the library – but rocks shouldn't be too difficult to brush up on. I've got to have this baby. It would hurt not to have it.

On the way here I thought I recognised the road, since I went to school nearby. But it was like in those cowboy films when there seem to be an awful lot of Indians falling off horses, but it's only the same Indian on the same old horse. I kept thinking I knew the next bend in the road, but I didn't. It was just like a thousand other roads bordered with green hedges and ribboned with grass, and the same old tree bending down. I remember one ride to school, in the dark, my very first term. I'd had my hair permanently waved and it had the same texture as my grey school coat. The bus turned off the road into a drive, and there were shapes of trees and a notice board showing faintly, and someone said we'd arrived. We ate egg on toast in a basement which might have been a dungeon, and there were long loaves of bread with wet insides, and most of the girls seemed elderly and lit cigarettes after the meal. One girl had bunches of yellow curls hanging like grapes above each ear. She wore a clever, amused expression, and after yawning she said, 'My God, I'm tired.' Then we walked in the darkness outside, under some trees and through a door that had horses' hooves nailed up all over it, and up some stone steps into a room with three beds. The girl with the clever face said I'd better make my bed, and another girl came in and began to eat an onion. I turned my back and fiddled with my bedding and looked at the name tapes my mother had sewn on the blankets, and tears came into my eyes because I didn't know how to make a bed, and I felt foolish and sad and not at all beautiful. I wasn't beautiful, but every day at the same time I said to God 'Please make me better looking', and that made my inside feel better. In the end I had to turn round, and the onion-eater said 'Aren't you the girl that's had no schooling?' in a funny sprawled voice – a South African take-me-back-to-the-old-Transvaal voice. I said, 'Yes.' She must have been mixing me up with someone else, because I'd hardly had a beastly day off school for years; but it was easier than saying I hadn't got a bed of my own at home and that I slept with my mother, and that she always made the bed anyway, and that my brother slept with my father. There were two empty bedrooms as well and we all slept without nightclothes, except my father, who wore cream combinations. If there had ever been a fire, God help us, we would all have had to burn rather than come down a ladder so unprepared, and if one of us went to the lavatory in the middle of the night Father would shout out, 'Many there, luv?' This girl, who was later quite nice, and who used to break into the Prince Igor dances at the drop of a hat (proving to me how lucky I was to possess greater sensitivity, seeing I was thinner than her but would have died rather than dance anything and show my muscular calves), helped me make the bed. The other girl lay back looking wrier than ever, and I thought

I'd better worry tomorrow over the misunderstanding about my former expensive education. There's very little about my schooldays I remember now, except the snow coming down one winter Sunday when we went to church. In the square the Salvation Army band was playing 'The Sea of Love is Rolling In'. It was a bit like a Christmas card, and I think I felt like crying. I don't mean I was homesick or anything. It's just that sentimental moments like that generally make me forget how special I could be if only I had the chance, and I get all lost and puny and dwindle right down to almost nothing. Anyway, I remember that particular morning because later, in church, I didn't kneel down quick enough, and Matron thwacked me on the shoulder with her umbrella, and I almost swung round and bashed her. Not that I minded too much about the umbrella, but I'd been daydreaming about the vicar, alternating between thinking he was Rochester and I was Jane Eyre (what, leave Ferndale and all that I hold most dear?) and the idea of him being Charles Boyer in that film about the Titanic. We were sinking together with the violins playing – and Matron spoilt it with her brolly tapping. I haven't mentioned to Edward that I went to school here, or about the vicar. Once or twice when I've told him little anecdotes about my past, he's given me a funny look. I'd like him to be jealous, but I don't want to overdo it. Men are funny like that – their way of showing jealousy is to disappear off the face of the earth.

I've told Norman about the school. He was impressed, I think, despite his being a Communist. Anyway, he didn't laugh, which was a blessing. His laugh is terrible; his nostrils flare like a horse. When I first heard him sniggering I was interviewing him about a room to rent in my house in Morpeth Street. I'm not really a Bloated Capitalist. The house had been left to me by my Auntie Edith, and it was falling down. Some of the windows were missing. There was only me living there, and Miss Evans, the hair-remover, who changed into gum boots and a mackintosh when she returned from work because the place was so damp. She carried a torch because she was afraid the light switches would give her a shock. She was over-cautious, but then her career in electrolysis had probably unnerved her. Someone had told me they knew a man who would be suitable as a lodger; he was clean and quiet and kept himself to himself. I needed the money, so I said he could come round and I'd talk to him. When I opened the door to him at our first meeting he appeared small and somehow old-fashioned. He had narrow trousers and wore a detachable collar with rounded edges, like the ones my father affected, and a flat peaked cap. He took his cap off and sort of bowed. There was a fire in my living-room. I was proud of that room. The wallpaper had a pattern of Sicilian lions with their tongues sticking out, and there was a brass bed and a piano, and the stuffed head of a moose on the wall with a paper garland twisted round its horns. It wasn't everybody's cup of tea, but that room had style. I felt very like a landlady, which I was, and I behaved very formally at the beginning. I started to say that I liked to be quiet, but Norman didn't stop at a distance to listen; he advanced closer and closer, neck stuck out like a tortoise above his wing collar, till we were nose to nose, and my skirt began to smoulder. Oh ho, I thought, this is a right one all right, and then he spun me round and beat at my bottom with his flat check cap. After he had come to live in the house he said he couldn't believe his luck – me catching fire like that. I said it was no wonder and did he always have to talk to one so intensely. He said he had wax in both ears and had to lip-read to understand what people were saying and that was why he moved so near. I did once get him to have the wax cleaned out, but for weeks afterwards he suffered terribly from all the cups rattling in the Kardomah, and the machines at work, and I had to buy him ear-plugs till the wax re-formed.

I haven't had much chance to talk to Norman this weekend. When we lived in the same house we used to talk for hours. We haven't even been able to discuss Shebah being shot in the leg. We won't ever be able to talk about it, not for ages. Norman will be going back up north and I'll be returning to my new bedsitter in London. It's a pity there's not more time. It's all so final, so serious. A crusade to end all crusades, in a sense. I don't really think it's *that* serious. Norman was going to tell me what he thought of Edward, whether he was suitable, but Shebah's accident got in the way. I think Edward will be all right. He is, after all, according to Claude, the reflection of the tenderness I bear myself. It's always ourselves we love, Claude says.

Yesterday, when we arrived and went through the door into the shop, Claude held his arms out so wide that there was no way to go but into them. At the moment of penetration into the shop, or partial penetration, because our embrace had piled the others into a heap behind, Victorian Norman trod on Shebah's foot, which lay exposed in an open-work sandal. She swore at him.

'Man,' said Claude, shaking Edward's hand, 'good to see you.' Then Julia said nice things, and we were through the shop, into the hall and going up the open staircase to the living-room above. A wooden angel tethered to the wall held praying hands above Shebah's Napoleonic pigtail.

'Oh my God,' she breathed.

I wanted to hug Edward – I wanted to stand on tiptoe and pirouette on the Indian carpet and show him everything at once – but I was torn by wanting to show Shebah and Victorian Norman too. I pointed quickly in all directions – the jade for Shebah, the Boucher nudes for Norman – and I brought my hand round past the piano and the glass and the silver in a sort of circle until I was pointing at myself. I suppose I really meant Edward to understand 'All this and me too'. Actually, it was wasted on him. He wasn't watching. Claude was, though, and he knew what I meant and I nearly shouted with laughter, though again I might have felt like crying. All this emotion is so wearying, as Shebah would put it. I think it's inherited. My father always wept when they played 'Silver Threads among the Gold' on the wireless.

Upstairs in Claude's room there was so much to look at and touch that for a while we didn't have to talk. Then Julia showed me into a bedroom with pink-washed walls and a china cherub with a pot belly holding up a lamp bulb, and she said, 'This room is for you and Edward. How are things? You look well.'

'I feel marvellous,' I told her. I did mean it. Loud laughter came from the living-room, and a sort of shivering sound as though someone had touched the harp.

Last time I came here, I saw Billie. He sat near the harp, he touched it with his knuckles and it lurched sideways. The flaps of his stupid flying helmet swung on either side of his face like a spaniel's ears. Everything in the room trembled – all the little glass things and the little china things: a thousand, tiny dying vibrations in the crowded room. It was Claude's idea that we should meet here. Neutral ground, he called it. Just talk to him, he told me. He said I might get Billie back if I found the right words. When it came to it, in spite of the years spent apart and the years spent together and the millions of words written on paper when Billie went away to Australia, all the words seemed the wrong ones. I remember in my head what he had written in letters –

> *'I think of you constantly. If I said, come out here to me, would you?*
>
> *'I sat on a balcony overlooking Sydney harbour, and watched the lights and thought of you. I drove into the bush last night. The gum trees sprawl in the dust. We shot a kangaroo later. When it was skinned there was a naked fleshless baby, not quite breathing. I thought of you.*
>
> *'How you would revel in this heat, how it would suit your unconventional ideas of summer dress . . .'*

I hadn't been able to begin to imagine what sort of heat he meant. Sometimes, when we had a warm day in the backyard of Morpeth Street, I had put sun oil on my stomach. Across my throat had spread a line of black specks, a necklace of sooty beads. I had lain on the paving stones unaware of just how pitiful, how callus-footed, how unbelievable I was. I didn't believe in heritage, in what is handed down – the curve of bone, the thickness of the skin – I thought everything was juxtaposed by brain and mind and lovely thoughts. And Billie told me the truth. Which I couldn't accept. I had to talk it out, I had to tell him something. He had to help me rebuild that image of myself he had so cruelly shattered. A knife thrust into the personality, Claude says, can lead to loss of life.

'I can't help it if I don't love you, can I?' Billie had said finally. 'I have been so ashamed of you, so embarrassed.'

'But I've been ill,' I told him. 'It was my father dying and the shock of you coming home.'

'It wouldn't work, you must see that,' he said. 'You would never fit in with my parents.'

I would have preferred a kick in the face, or a removal of my front teeth. 'I suppose really I never really loved you,' I lied.

He spun round. For an instant he was the old lovely, sentimental Billie . . . 'But I loved you,' he said.

We didn't say anything else. We can lose actualities, Claude says, but to have dreams torn from us is too much.

The vintage car, the one Billie and I had made love in, went out of the yard. Billie's face at the wheel seemed so cheerful. He waved, he touched the cap on his head. A thin trail of exhaust rose in the warm air. There was nothing more to do but hunch my shoulders and bow low to protect my damaged heart. I went for a walk along the road with Claude and cried out at each tree, because there was no one to hear, and Claude put his arm round my shoulders (already not drooping quite so much) and a chill breeze made us walk faster and faster.

I don't know why I'm so stuck on Billie. Maybe it had a lot to do with my mother. She liked him – you could say she encouraged him. She thought because he wore a bowler hat he must be a gentleman. She invited him to supper, and she didn't bat an eyelid when he stroked my leg under the table. It was quite obvious what he was doing, because I went bright red. She had practically screamed when the hotel waiter had put his arm round my shoulder; she thought hotel waiters were common. My father didn't like Billie. I've got a photograph of my dad as a child in knickerbockers, taken after a board-school concert in the year dot, when he sang 'Lily of Laguna': he has a weird expression on his face, as though there was something nasty jumping out of the camera at him. He looked at Billie in the same sort of way – though, come to think of it, that was his normal expression.

The first time Billie ever took me out we went to a charity night at the Empire Theatre. During a selection from *Rose Marie*, I was sick. Most of it went over Billie's trousers. He dragged me out of the auditorium. All the retching sounds echoed up and down the stone corridor. I'm not usually sick; I think Billie made me nervy. After that we didn't go out much. When I moved into Auntie Edith's house we played ping-pong in the evenings, on a small table. Billie didn't actually live with me, in case my mother dropped in and accused me of being a whore. He stayed most nights, though. Shebah hated him. She kept telling me she'd met him before in compromising circumstances – at a poetry group, at a drama meeting, somewhere very unlikely. 'It's not possible,' I said, but when they came face to face in the kitchen you could tell she recognised him, though Billie denied knowing her from Adam. He was probably telling the truth. Shebah's one of those people who once seen are never forgotten. She wears bright red lipstick and her upper lip is quite hairy. Most people refuse to walk down the street with her. Norman says she looks like a demented nun, but I think she's more like a crazed pirate. Coming here, Norman refused to travel with her. He put her on the London train and then walked away. She was wailing, he said, and waving all her scarves. Until this weekend she'd always vowed she would never go on a train because of sitting with all the scum, and yet the idea of travel appeals to her. At one time we discussed the possibility of her making a permanent life for herself on the railways – at night, when she wouldn't see so many people. 'Living is what gets me, darling,' she said, 'but if I could move about sitting down, and just see things through windows without being observed, it would be splendid.' Actually she desires people like some people desire money or fame. Through people,

Claude says, she transcends her ageing body. She's over sixty now, and I don't think she's ever looked any different. She has a photograph in her handbag of herself as a girl on a charabanc outing, and even then there was a shadow above her top lip. Claude says her conception of herself, the young bosoms bobbing on the waves, the plump shoulders touched by the sea at Blackpool, is based on a snapshot taken forty years ago. She thinks other women are out to get her.

'If I really bothered, darling,' she often tells me, 'if I really cared to dress up, darling, they'd kill me with their jealousy. Oh God, they'd smother me with their bloody rotten jealousy.'

Actually I think she was jealous of Billie. She resented his being in my house, spending hours with me which should have been given to her. Shebah had all the time in the world. She still has. When I used to tell her to go home she'd stall for time, talking and fidgeting, leaning in mock exhaustion against the wall, festooned with her parcels and carrier bags. She always carried a little bit of fish for tomorrow, and last Sunday's paper folded at the theatre criticism, and a quarter pound of wurst in an envelope. She detested my opening the front door and helping her down the steps. She clutched at the railings like a suffragette, determined not to let go, her fish and her paper and her wurst falling among the milk bottles. She knew when I shut the front door that I would pelt back up the hall to Billie with my arms open. She was overjoyed when he skedaddled to Australia, because then there were nights when I would call her back and tell her she could stay. I liked her. She's good company. We drank stewed tea. When we went to bed she told me to turn my back while she removed her boots, her two coats and her three cardigans tied round the waist with darning wool. I slept on the sofa. I thought it was more dignified for her, being old, to have the bed to herself. She groaned as she hauled herself on to the brass bed, shrieked with laughter as she lay half in and half out, called on God for help, damned all her bloody relations, and coughed as the rain beat against the broken windows. Regularly at two in the morning, Victorian Norman used to walk, as if up a rock face, along the hall and into the kitchen for his clock. We heard his muttered chat to the automatic time exchange . . . 'Thank you . . . Ta very much'; then the sound of the clock being wound, the locking of the kitchen door, an explosive cry of rage from the brass bed (nothing articulate); then two sets of snoring, one loud, a foot or so away from me, one faint, coming from the recumbent Norman, stark naked and arms flung wide on the truckle bed in the room above.

Norman's fond of her too, even if he won't travel with her. They're a bit alike, the way they think. Or rather, the way they've both been schooled in the University of Life. That's what Norman calls it. He's awfully clever. You'd never think he worked in a factory. He never stops reading, and his mind's very active. He's always quoting things at me. His reaction to what I tried to do after Billie came back from Australia was strange. I thought he'd be kind to me and show lots of sympathy, but he said I was stupid. He didn't even seem glad I'd survived. I don't suppose I really meant to die. I just wanted a bit of peace. I remember going to see *Peter Pan* when I was small and thinking how weird it was when Peter said to the lost boys that to die must be an awfully big adventure. I didn't like it when my father died. I didn't even know he was poorly, though I thought he ate too much and took too little exercise. When my mother rang me up and said he was dead, it didn't seem like an adventure at all. The funeral was terrible. I nearly missed it because it was foggy and the trains were late.

On the way to the church the hearse kept vanishing in the fog. At the kerb, four men in black took my father away in his wooden box and bore him off into the mist. It was a shock, bent in the pew, to straighten up and see the coffin, such a little coffin, right alongside me near the altar rails. It was made of white wood and had a wreath of flowers on top. The flowers were supposed to be from me and my mother, but I hadn't contributed anything to them because I hadn't any money. The vicar spoke a lot of words about how cheerful my father was and how he always had a cheerful word for everyone (God forgive him for the years and years of never speaking). He omitted to mention that my father suffered from severe melancholia at least once a month; nor did he mention the misery he caused my mother, the long evenings she sat in the bedroom with red eyes, the sugar bowl dented because it had missed her and hit the wall behind, the smashed window in the hall ('The blitz, you know. Surprising, isn't it?'). My mother cried noisily, her snuffles fanning out the veil of her hat. The deaf man in the coffin lay with his feet pointing at the vaulted roof. Many a time we'd rolled cursing in each other's arms on the kitchen floor, each of us struggling to get the upper hand, me trying to bash his head on the fender because he made my mother cry, and he spitting out that I was a little bastard, a filthy animal with no respect, a dirty little beast who should have died in the grass. My mother generally hid if there was a row, but eventually she'd come downstairs and she'd say, 'Don't upset yourself, my pet. Run out into the garden and play.' She never said that at the funeral. After the vicar's speech, the church doors opened and the four men swooped to lift my father up. Fog rolled like a carpet down the aisle. We followed the coffin, one foot after the other, tracking him, the procreator of my hooked nose, my skeleton of bones. How sad it was, how dark it was! The organ music was pretty mournful; I'd have preferred them to play 'Lily of Laguna' as they carried him towards the grave. I'm sorry he's gone. I think babies ought to have grandfathers, I expect he would have known how to be loving second time round.

It was nothing to do with my father, me wanting to get married and have this baby. I'm more scared of my mother than I ever was of him. I'd like to win her approval and have a wedding. I've led rather a rackety life and it's not much fun for her; neighbours are always leaning over the fence and asking her, 'How's your Lily? Not married yet, I suppose?' She probably tells them I've got better things to do, but she's upset about it, I know, and if I don't settle down soon she'll stop going out altogether and she'll draw the curtains against the world. She'd do it to spite me. And really I haven't anything better to do. I never had. I expect that's what drove Billie away to Australia. He wasn't brave enough to say right out that he didn't consider me suitable to be his wife. He said we'd have a house in the country and we'd get a dog for our children, and all the time he was talking about the dog and nice things like that he was enquiring about tin-mines, and sending off for emigration papers. During that first year, after he'd gone, he only wrote every three months or so. I thought it was very good of him. *Suspect goodness above all things*, Victorian Norman says. But then later, in the middle of the second year, Billie wrote to me every day – love letters – and he asked me to marry him. I'm glad I had the sense not to tell my mother and raise her hopes needlessly. Thinking about it, I imagine it wasn't sense that stopped me, but disbelief.

The night before Billie returned from Australia, Victorian Norman watched me try on some clothes.

'How did he use to like you?' he asked.

'Oh, sort of arty, I think,' I said.

Once I had a white coat like a smock and Billie had said in the street, 'Oh my little Rose of Sharon, O my little pretty.' Maybe he didn't. He did sometimes say I looked nice.

I tried on a check skirt and a striped sweater. Victorian Norman shook his head above his starched collar. 'No, not really,' he said.

I tried on a brown and black dress, very tight and split under one armpit. Norman liked it; he liked the split arm-piece and the frilled petticoat that hung down.

'He'll think it a bit messy,' I said, and I took it off. 'I've got to appear as if I've made an effort but am really not superficial or made up, just the old eternal child of nature I ever was.'

Norman laughed and went on reading his paper.

Nothing seemed the thing to wear. Reflected in the blotched mirror over the sink, my face looked empty – or maybe it was my face that was blotchy. I had two lines on my forehead, just above my nose, as if I had frowned for two years.

'Why didn't I go to bed early?' I asked Norman, looking at the dark circles under my eyes.

Later I put 'Party Doll' on the gramophone and twisted my hips. But suddenly neither of us was convinced, because all the other nights when we had made a noise and played the oldest records (why did they all have meaningful titles – 'I'll Never Make the Same Mistake Again', 'Sweetheart', 'Somewhere in France with You', 'Silver Threads among the Gold') the mornings had been predictable and tomorrow wasn't. It wasn't going to be an ordinary day. I went to bed without washing properly, and before I turned out the light I kissed the photographed face of Billie. And truly I think I did feel optimistic. I did feel safe and happy and hopeful.

The following evening at six-thirty I was washed and ready for him. A fire burnt in the grate beneath the Sicilian lions; the brass bed under its white coverlet glittered in the firelight. At the table in the kitchen I arched my eyebrows and folded my hands together on the lap of my dark plaid skirt, watching the shadow of the lampshade twist round and back again above the blue oilcloth. There was new lino on the floor, carried painfully all the way from the shop two days before, an outsize roll of black-and-white squares, oily under the rain. There were new curtains on the windows, white ones hemmed with blue cotton and drawn against a backyard under a layer of soot and a row of cats on a high brick wall. On the balcony of the house next door the husband threw washing-up water in a flood down the wooden steps and lost the bucket in a welter of noise. Two chops in silver paper, garnished and rubbed with garlic, lay on the draining board. I'd prepared a pan of sliced potatoes under water and there were two packets of frozen vegetables, one yellow, one green, to give colour to the white plates painted with columbine. The most important thing, Shebah had told me two days before, was the expression reflected and transferred from the eye at the first moment of meeting. Let him know who you are, she said, and let him know where you are. I am here, I told myself, but who am I?

A knock shattered the house; through the keyhole I spied the returned Colonial Boy, outline blurred behind the glass, raising an arm to smooth his hair. Cold air rushed in as the door opened; all I could see was a coat, a check coat, clean and alien. The coat came into the house.

How was I to know that the sun would have made him brown, bleached the line of hair on his cheekbone, paled the nails that tipped his fingers? His palms opened and showed cream as he handed me a package.

'Go on, open it,' he said. 'It's for you.'

Inside the tissue paper was a box, a small jewel box with velvet backing. To the accompaniment of suitable music from a dream film, shot close up to show the dewy eyes of a girl looking at her very first engagement ring, mouth curved in a tender smile, someone, me, picked out the toffee laid so carefully inside the box. I unwrapped it and placed the sticky sweet upon my thick and waiting tongue. Like a consecrated wafer it stayed in my mouth. My lips wouldn't close. I turned to the meat, bloody on its silver foil, and lit the grill.

'You've been here all this time?' Billie asked. His eyes took in the dirt, the line of grease above the cooker, the cobwebs on the ceiling. With the grilling of the chops, the twisting of the red-fringed shade above the oilcloth on the table, love flickered, struggled to evoke some past echo of delight and began wholly to be extinguished. Still I fought for something, some period of reprieve, eyes down to the spitting fat, not looking at my executioner, my pen-friend, my blue-eyed bully-boy in the beautiful coat.

'I left my cases at the station,' he said. 'I ought to be thinking about looking for a hotel.'

I didn't believe him. The striped sheets on the brass bed were laundry-fresh. I couldn't reply, I couldn't breathe. At last we reached the bedroom with the fire – only the fire was nearly out and I hadn't the heart to put more coal on, and he kept looking at everything. And when I looked too, at each picture, at each article of furniture, the brass candlesticks on the mantelshelf, the brass samovar, the stuffed owl in its case in the alcove, nothing shone any more, nothing gleamed, everything bore fingerprints of neglect. The filigree neck of the samovar was cracked, the glass eyes of the moth-eaten moose stared dully at the Sicilian lions. The whole room was a monument to despair.

'You look tired,' he said.

Dumbly I prepared for the night. I found my face-cream and sat at the table. I was trying to be natural. 'Hold the mirror for me,' I said.

With each circlet of grease I rubbed away one more layer of romantic love and sat exposed with shining nose and oily mouth, suburban, self-tormenting, waiting to be hurt. I moved towards the cupboard to put my jar away, parodying those other figures moving at night across his two years of travelling, those golden girls fresh from showers who raised slender arms to push away their damp, bleached hair.

At last he said, 'Your ankles are thick.'

'Thanks for telling me,' I said.

'I'll come back first thing in the morning,' said Billie.

'Yes,' I said.

'I'll be very tender,' said Billie suddenly, bending down to kiss me.

In a welter of cloth, in a smother of check overcoat, with an adroit convulsive roll a penetration unpremeditated and untender took place. There was toffee in my teeth. He wore his coat all night. It might have been a coat that opened and sheltered me. I could have lain warm within it, if he'd bothered to unbutton it.

In the morning I went out to buy some bacon for his breakfast and when I returned to the house he'd gone, and Norman sat stricken, and the turtle's back had gone out of the hall, and the brass horn from the piano top, and I never saw him at the house again. Victorian Norman did. Billie came back for his boxing gloves when I was in hospital. He said I had deteriorated physically and that he preferred me as I was before. Then he and Norman shook hands and Billie went down the hall as he had done so many times in the past, only this time I wasn't there to put my arms about his shambling waist, and out he went, never to return. Positively a last appearance, if indeed it was he who had returned in the first place. He left behind nothing, nothing beyond the new lino in the kitchen and the new curtains already turning a rich grey. Of course, that's what I thought at the time. I never guessed what he'd left behind, in me. And if I'd known, I wouldn't have done what I did. I don't remember planning it.

I sat at the kitchen table, the blue oilcloth franked by the ringed impressions of a dozen mugs of tea, my head in my arms, and I waited. On the table was the bacon I'd bought and one large empty bottle of gin, purchased duty free at the bar of Billie's homecoming ship. I only wanted to sleep, to cease upon the midnight with no pain. I heard a sound from the telephone, like the buzzing of a fly trapped behind glass. I remember picking up the receiver and hearing a voice repeating my name, making a persistent enquiry, until with boredom, because it wasn't Billie's voice, I dropped the earpiece with a dull plastic thud on a white square of lino, the third from the closed and paper-choked door, and fell beastlike on all fours. I slid finally, the toes of my winkle-picker shoes curled up, cheek to cheek with the cool surface of the floor, one finger held up for silence in the small groove under my nose which Claude says is the imprint of God's finger in the wet clay. With mouth clumsily ajar, first with a gentle soughing of air, then with a frantic galloping of hooves, I went into a long cave of dreamless sleep. I suppose it was wicked of me; my friends would have missed me and my mother would have cried.

Claude told me I must never tell Billie what I'd done, but I did. After all, I've never attempted anything as big as that in my whole life, and it should have made Billie proud. Not everybody knows somebody who'd die for them. Anyway, it didn't work, and that's why this weekend is terrifically important to me. I wish I didn't have to lie to Edward. It would be so nice if the baby were really his, and I could have told him the news as a sort of birthday present. He was twenty-nine yesterday. Last night Julia cooked a celebration dinner. Shebah was cross at us for making a fuss over Edward. She thinks any admiration or affection should be directed towards her. We drank bottles and bottles of wine.

'It's a bloody marvellous life,' said Norman, and he hit Edward on the back in friendly fashion. Edward is a man of few words. He just grunted. Shebah, of course, said life was rotten. We were all swine, she said. She didn't know what Norman found so marvellous about living.

'I drink,' shouted Norman, 'I copulate.' He was only trying to annoy Shebah. She hates sex being mentioned, particularly when she's eating.

'I reckon you're right,' said Claude. 'I reckon that Edward here should cleave to this woman.' He held the bottle towards Edward. 'More wallop, man?'

'No, no more,' said Edward.

'I should have brought my hat,' I said, lolling weakly against his shoulder so that he would feel I belonged to him. I began telling him about the hat I wear on festive occasions. 'I wore it,' I said, 'when that policeman was calling and chaining his bike to the railings, and when we all went to the club, and that night you came, Claude, and you wore that Indian frock coat that somebody left behind . . .'

'Ah, that little blonde,' cried Claude, 'going with me to the chippie for those Chinese roll things . . . such a dear sweet thing. She thought I was a priest.'

Victorian Norman wriggled on his chair. He remembered the blonde with delight.

'She got attacked the night of my father's funeral,' I said. I started to mention the fog but trailed off, because of Edward. I wasn't sure whether he'd appreciate my being jokey about a funeral, about my Papa, about my little plantation weed with the cheekbones and the stained homburg hat.

Claude understood my problem. His head wagged, and a globule of red wine shook from his gold beard and stained the cloth. I had to look away. Julia put the kettle on. Edward looked embarrassed and lit another cigarette.

'We'll make a night of it,' said Claude, looking at me.

'If you don't mind,' said Edward, pushing back his chair and standing upright, 'I'd like to spend the beginning of my birthday in bed.'

Not even Shebah laughed. We looked at him, and I said, 'Of course,' and he said good night politely to them all and bent his head to go through the low door into the shop.

'I reckon,' said Claude, 'that one's all right.'

I sat for five minutes feeling womanly and important, and smiling at everything, and when I left them to go upstairs Victorian Norman was standing at the sink with his arm round Julia. Shebah and Claude had their heads together in a parody of the rustic china lovers on the wall.

Edward was in bed, leaning on one elbow, watching me come through the door.

'Happy birthday,' I said.

'I love you, I love you,' he said.

'Here's your present,' I said. 'Change it if you don't like it.'

I laid the striped shirt on the coverlet.

'It's just perfect,' he said.

'Many happy returns.'

'I love you. Please, I love you,' he told me.

I was worried in case his lighted cigarette burned the blankets while we kissed.

'Let me go and do my teeth,' I said.

I could hear the others talking and Shebah shouting downstairs as I washed. I didn't know what to do. I kept remembering what Victorian Norman had said I must do, and I kept thinking I must do it, and yet I wished I could just tell the truth. There was an awful lot of hot water, but I felt Edward might be hurt if I took too much time washing, so I just rinsed my face and put some of Julia's perfume behind my ears, and some on my stomach, and combed my hair. Then I went back and got into bed and Edward switched off the light. Once the light went out I felt as if I was wrapped in cotton wool and a million miles from anyone.

Edward touched my cheek gently. 'It's a lovely shirt. It really is a nice shirt. Thank you.'

My cheek clung to his shoulder, damp with heat. My eyes stared into the darkness.

'Is it really your collar size, Edward?' I asked.

His hand stroked my hair to ease my disappointment. 'Well, not really,' he said. 'But it doesn't matter, really it doesn't.'

'You're sure?' I said.

'We could frame it and put it on the mantelpiece,' he suggested.

We laughed. He wrapped his arms about me, and I felt very cheerful. Surely he was implying that it would be *our* mantelpiece. I was so grateful I nearly told him about Billie, only I knew at the end it would have left me anxious for physical contact and Edward would have been withdrawn and miserable.

And Victorian Norman had told me I mustn't tell him, not ever, if I wished this time to be peaceful.

'Why are you crying?' Edward touched my eyelids with his fingers – which felt like paper and smelt of tobacco – and I said, 'Because I'm happy.' Which was the truth. I can't help my ephemeral emotions. I decided long ago that it is my greatest weakness, this inability to sustain any sense of misery. I'm like the bubbles in a glass of fizzy lemonade. I keep rising to the top.

'So am I. You make me happy,' said Edward.

Outside the room a chorus began. 'Happy birthday to you, happy birthday to you, happy birthday, dear Edward . . . '

There was a great deal of laughing, of shuffling. Someone, Claude of course, began to turn the door handle. I laughed loudly to let them know that it was a great joke, spluttering my appreciation against Edward's shoulder. Over the noise Julia said, 'No, Claude, no', and they moved away still singing, a little band of happy wanderers.

'They do mean it kindly,' I told the silent Edward in the darkness – though of course they didn't, at least not Claude. Not unkindly either. It was just that they wanted to protect me, most of all from myself. Faintly I heard Shebah singing, 'Let's start all over again, let us be sweethearts once more.' It's one of her favourite songs. Usually she dances to it. At the last two lines she always gathers up her short skirts in her hands, lifts one plump shoulder and shouts, almost in tears, 'Though the fault was mine, to forgive is divine . . . ' Then there's a pause, a coquettish flutter of eyelashes, and a sideways canter into imaginary wings . . . 'So let's start all over again.'

Edward stubbed out his cigarette and I muttered 'Happy birthday' into his ear, kissing his face all over, until he buried me under love, and I went willingly enough, knowing how important it was to the future.

From a distance I heard Norman's laugh as he went into the bathroom. I said into the darkness, 'I do love you, you know.'

And Edward replied, 'Then it's all right, it's all right, love.'

I felt calm and a bit bumptious and I had to turn away from him lest I cling to him and spoil everything. And what would I do then, poor thing, poor thing.

Being calm was like looking at an aerial landscape – very silent, with a network of little roads and hedges and rivers, and trees bunched like fists and saddles of pines flung over hills, and small stone walls separating handkerchief fields – everything little and geometrical and in each square groups of people moving: parents and relations and the hotel waiter, and Shebah and Victorian Norman, and Billie in a matchbox car and, alone near a river, myself, looking up with pebble eyes. It was so ordered and on such a graspable scale that I felt that the pattern of my life wasn't so complicated after all. All I had to do was to step over into another field and somebody would hold my hand.

In the next room I could hear Shebah still singing. Very carefully I moved out of one side of the visitors' bed, and stood listening to make sure Edward was asleep. I went to the bathroom to comb my hair. I put up a hand and pulled the light cord. There was me in the mirror opposite, round-shouldered and hook-nosed, and Victorian Norman and Julia in an embrace. Norman's laugh billowed out and Julia moved her hands blindly across the wash basin, reaching for her glasses. Almost at once Claude came into the bathroom. He reached out and held me against his shirt front. 'Nice time, dear one,' he said, and smiled fondly while his blue eyes took in Julia's pink face. Two buttons were undone at the neck of her cream blouse. 'Good God, girl,' he said, very quietly, and I knew exactly what he meant and nothing was solved after all.

After a time one has to pretend that certain things matter in order to appear normal – it's all so feeble. Julia was upset, I could tell. She followed Claude worriedly out of the doorway. I combed my hair, and Victorian Norman went on rubbing at the toothpaste stains on the glass, shrugging his shoulders up and down to compose himself. I didn't speak, knowing how he hates immediate discussion and that his mind would be full of thoughts of what he would have done and what he might have done if he hadn't been interrupted. He started to whistle, very shrilly, the tune of 'Sussex-by-the-Sea'. Then we went into the living-room, and he stroked my bottom just as we entered. I leaped almost on top of Shebah, who stood, still singing, braceleted arms stretched out to an invisible audience near the gramophone. She stopped in the middle of a note, and said, 'Oh darling', sadly, and entreatingly, as if she thought I shouldn't be there. Claude gave me a drink and a ciggie and I sat with my feet curled up under my pink striped nightgown. Because of Billie I'll never willingly show my ankles again.

'What's happened, darling?' demanded Shebah. 'Are you all right, darling?'

There we sat all together – Julia was in the bedroom repairing her lipstick – graduates of the University of Life, three of us immoral, cynical and lost, and Shebah, the music-hall nun, mad for half a lifetime, emitting signals of sensitivity. Victorian Norman was listening respectfully to Claude, who was talking about his departed Sarah. 'There was real glory, man,' he repeated, 'real glory.' Claude and I smiled at each other across the room as Shebah moved between us and stood peering down at me in the lap of the velvet chair.

'It's no good, darling,' she said, 'you can't deceive me.' Her eyes, bulging like marbles, searched my face for some sign of distress, some explanation as to why I had left my bridal bed. Her fat hand came down with a shiver of bangles, to test whether my forehead were hot to the touch.

'I'm all right, Shebah,' I said. 'Edward fell asleep, and I thought I would like a cigarette.'

When Julia came back into the room, with adjusted hair and freshly painted mouth, Shebah concentrated on her. She stood, hand on hip, talking to Julia, glancing at me from time to time, her rubber lips stretching and spitting out sounds, looking like some welfare worker explaining the blanket situation to her second-in-command. I might have been an evacuee waiting to be billeted. With all the drinking and smoking I felt a bit hysterical, so I shut my eyes tight, and there was an image of Billie's check coat. It was as if a hand had suddenly caught my heart and squeezed it. I dug my teeth into my lip and asked myself over and over, 'Who are you? What's your name? Don't lie. What's the full name?' ... until gradually the squeezing stopped and little by little my heart filled out again. It wasn't exactly unpleasant. There was a kind of pained elation I wanted to share, so I opened my eyes, but neither Claude nor Victorian Norman was in the room and Shebah, who anyway only responds when grief is secretive, had her back to me. After a while I went down the wooden stairs, under the flying angel at prayer, and through the shop to the backyard scented with leaves. Broken statues lay in the grass. It was too cold to go very far. Anyway, I wanted to be noticed. I'm useless when I'm not noticed.

I sat down at a wrought-iron table and heard a funny noise like someone pumping up a tyre. It was Claude, stripped to the waist, wielding a spray filled with insecticide. 'I reckon the thing to do is submit,' he said.

'There's not much else I can do,' I agreed. I didn't really know what he meant, but that's not important with Claude. 'Have you managed to have a talk with him yet?' I asked. 'Have you told him nice things about me?'

'Wait and see,' he said. He sent another cloud of spray into the night air before coming to sit on the wooden bench by the table. A moth, feeble in a ray of light from the upper windows of the house, fluttered above our heads.

'It won't be great glory, my love,' said Claude insanely, rubbing a fold of skin pouched from the barrel of his ribs. 'However, it will be a solution.' He raised his eyes to the windows above and informed me, 'Edward has just gone from bed to bog for the third time.'

'I'll go up presently,' I said.

'I should,' he replied.

His fingers lay motionless across my feet. I leaned my jaw against my knees and sniffed my own musk smell. It's odd how other people's smells are awful and your own's all right. Unless you really like someone.

It was nice sitting there, but something was wrong. There was a feeling of strain at the roof of my mouth, as if I'd started to yawn but forgotten to complete the act. When I looked at the wistaria with its twisted stem clinging to the centre wall of the house, leaves shifted – and there was Billie's coat again, made out of fingers of light, black and white, with three round moving buttons. I can't actually see the coat if I try to imagine it, but it's always there when I don't expect it. The coat isn't a noun, it's almost a verb. It's *I coat* and *You coat*, though it's difficult to explain, most of all to myself. Fortunately I'm so superficial by nature that in time I expect I'll stop thinking about it.

I didn't sleep very well. Nor, I believe, did Edward. Several times I awoke and he wasn't there.

Victorian Norman slept on the sofa in the living-room. When I saw him this morning, he was still asleep. A dog, the one with the white face, was sharing his bed. On the threshold of Shebah's room I stepped over a scrap of orange scarf and trod on something sharp, like glass. Shebah was stretched on a camp bed, the black circumference of her beret showing above an army blanket, her grey pigtail sticking out like a skein of wool. She was groaning softly. Suddenly she cried out, 'What shall I do?'

'What's up, my dove?' I asked.

She said in desperate tones, 'Oh darling, the damage I've done,' and wailed again, this time weakly.

I was trying to fathom it out when Claude came in carrying tea on a tin tray. He sat heavily on the side of the camp bed.

'What's the matter with Shebah?' I whispered, and he replied in that firm voice he uses when something is wrong but he intends to minimise it, 'Oh, we had a little accident. Nothing too bad, my love. Tea, Shebah?' He pushed the buttocks of the moaning Shebah, who heaved suddenly and tragically from beneath her army blanket, head of fire like John the Baptist, eyes rolling. Sobs shook the room. I made out the words, 'So sorry . . . so valuable . . . it's no use, darling . . . nothing is of any use . . . all life is a cheat . . . the prizes given at the children's party . . . ' and then her head ducked again and only the woolly tail of hair was exposed to view.

'We had just a little too much wine and a little too much starting all over again,' Claude said. 'She fell into the glass cabinet by the fireplace and there was a little broken glass.'

'All those china things,' I said. My mouth stayed open. After all, Shebah was my friend, my liability.

'No,' said Claude. 'Only one or two things, and one was something I'd mended before anyway, so not to worry.' He poured out the tea. 'How did it go, the birthday night?' he asked.

'All right,' I said. 'What about Julia?'

He shrugged. 'All right too.'

We fell silent, just looking at each other. The point about me and Claude is that having talked so much in the past we no longer need to say anything.

Shebah stopped crying. One eye, lit with a fearful glint of mock repentance, blinked over the hem of the sheet. Claude shouted, 'That's better, me dear, have a cup of tea,' and he put the mug by her side and went out into the living-room.

'Darling,' said Shebah, in a stage whisper that could be heard in the next room and the one beyond, 'it's dreadful, it's just dreadful. I tripped on the rug last night and fell against Claude's cabinet with all those beautiful pieces inside, and the glass broke and several things fell against each other and got chipped, and Julia said "Oh Christ", and you know how charming she is, and Claude never said a word, he just went on talking to Norman, and I felt terrible. I tried to see what damage I'd done and Claude bellowed across at me "Leave it, Shebah", very fierce, and Julia was then quite nice to me, but I felt like dying. I wish I'd never come.' She gave a loud hysterical laugh and I said, 'Oh, it's all right, love, everything's insured,' and again she laughed, more her old self, and stuffed one hand into her mouth to smother the hilarity that was shaking the bed.

I went into the living-room to see just how bad the damage was. Apart from a star-shaped hole in the front of the cabinet and some small pieces of glass that lay in the pile of the carpet, there was nothing.

I looked to see whether Edward was awake. The tea-bearing Claude was there also, sitting sideways on the nuptial bed, holding Edward by one arm. For my benefit Claude said loudly, 'Stick to her, there's great glory,' and Edward smiled a little uneasily and held the sheet against his vast unclothed shoulders with fingers stained brown with nicotine.

'Hallo, Edward,' I said, and Claude went out with his tray, this time looking for Victorian Norman.

I told Edward about Shebah, and he looked concerned. There was a little silence, until he said, 'A lot of things happened last night.' I suppose he meant us. I do love Edward – or will do soon.

When I was getting my clothes on he stared at my stomach. I don't know why. I nearly said something like 'Do you realise I may very well be pregnant after last night's carry-on?' – only I couldn't say it because I didn't know how he'd react. He was looking thoughtful. When I patted my tummy it was quite flat really. We went downstairs and through the shop and out into the back garden among the statues, and the sun was shining. We kissed beneath the trees. There was dew on the grass beyond the courtyard, and a bird sang on two notes.

'Coooeeee, darling,' called Shebah. She sounded quite cheerful. Then suddenly I heard a gun being fired and, following the bright ping of sound, maniacal laughter. Claude was in the open window of the living-room, an air rifle tucked into his shoulder, sunlight spilling off its metal barrel. He was leaning far out, one eye screwed up as he took aim.

A low moan rose from the grass a yard away from where we stood, and there lay Shebah, a fallen black crow, lying with powdered cheeks crushing the daisies. No one moved. Then there was another shot, and Victorian Norman ran over the grass towards us, hissing 'Lie down, the bugger's gone mad.' Obediently we fell down. Norman was laughing, and sweat was running down the side of his nose.

Then came Julia's voice, impatient: 'But Claude, they're all out there in the garden.'

Claude shouted innocently, with just the right shade of concern, 'Nobody hit, eh, man?'

At which Edward jumped to his feet and called back loudly, 'Yes, you've shot Shebah.'

Shebah was lying on her side, one Edwardian leg bent at the knee, the fingers of her right hand stretched starwise. I knelt unbelievingly, and one eye snapped open and fixed me with a look of hatred. 'The dirty rotten Jew-baiter,' she said, and quickly struggled to cover her exposed knee. When we got her upright and dusted the soil off her and poured the thimbleful of whisky between her sullen lips, she was beginning to enjoy herself. The damage was superficial after all. A pellet had merely hit one of the statues by the fence and ricocheted without much force on to Shebah's ankle. It hadn't lodged in the flesh, merely struck and trickled into the grass.

Julia put a bandage over the mark, on top of her stocking. Shebah grimaced throughout and groaned and bit her drooping lip and cast comical glances at us all. We put her on the wrought-iron bench just outside the back door on the paving stones, under the wistaria, with a stool to prop up her injured leg, and a travelling rug wrapped round her: she looked like a passenger on a veteran car rally. I kissed her cheek and felt that after the china breakages she probably felt better for being shot at, less under an obligation to Claude. She ate a big lunch and

Claude for his part seemed to present her with the tastier bits off the ham. It will give her something to remember, something concrete, personal, to add to her list of Jewish persecution.

Meanwhile we lie here waiting to go to the bus stop to make the return journey. I could find it in my heart to wish there was no return. As Victorian Norman says, the mind boggles. Claude is going to take a photograph of us before we go. I like photos of me and people I know. I'm a lucky girl to be surrounded by friends.

3

'She looks an interesting sort of girl,' said the man.

Claude didn't reply. He stared out into the yard, at the small garden beyond the barn where Lily and the others had posed for the photograph. 'Hurry, Claude,' she'd said, 'we don't want to miss that bus.' Shebah, surprisingly, hadn't minded the camera – had minded it less, in fact, than the isolated Edward, who had deliberately chosen to ignore Lily's hand reaching to hold his. Apart from the proximity of their fingers there was nothing to show that she had tried to reach him.

'Lily's always in some sort of trouble,' said Julia, 'but she has amazing resilience.' She stacked the empty cups on the draining board and put away the sugar and the biscuits. 'I have the greatest admiration for her,' she added, not quite sincerely.

'What sort of trouble?' The man had forgotten for the moment that he wanted to leave.

'Well, it's a bit difficult really to explain,' said Julia. 'She had several unhappy love affairs. Then she met a man called Billie and got pregnant.'

'Oh, that sort of trouble,' the man said, and saw that his wife was looking at him.

'Is Billie in the photograph?' she asked.

'No, he went away before he knew Lily was pregnant. He went away once before to Australia, but he came back again. Then she met someone else who wanted to marry her.'

'How convenient.' For some reason the woman sounded angry. 'So she's all right,' she added, listening to the bitterness in her own voice.

'Lily will never be all right,' said Claude.

'Do you really know that?' said Julia. 'Or do you mean it's inevitable?'

The woman was surprised at that particular question. She supposed that people living together must influence each other, though she herself didn't feel influenced in the slightest by her husband. But then they never talked about anything complicated. But that wasn't right. Nobody at this moment was discussing anything complicated. She frowned and said, 'I do think there's a lot of immorality these days,' and floundered, regretting something. 'I mean, an awful lot of people just put up with things. They don't give in.' She saw that her husband was staring at her, as if she had betrayed him, as if she had meant that *they* were merely putting up with each other.

'There aren't any people who put up with things,' said Claude. 'There are only people who have neither the opportunity nor the need.' When he turned round from the sink he was smiling. 'If you've never been in the position of either Lily or myself,' he went on, 'you can hardly know whether giving in applies.'

'You must admit,' said the man, feeling liberated by the sudden friendliness apparent in Claude, 'that there's an awful lot of letting go these days.'

'There's not enough,' said Claude cheerfully, taking the photograph from Julia. 'Mind you, we let go a bit that weekend, didn't we, girl?' He put an arm round Julia's waist and she leaned against him.

'It was a nice weekend,' she said.

She looked down at the snapshot into the face of Victorian Norman. 'You might have shown it me before,' she said mildly. 'I didn't even know you'd had it developed.'

But Claude had gone out of the kitchen and was in the front room of the shop attempting to clear a place for the newly bought plates. It was a pity, he thought, that there wasn't time to get to know everyone.

He couldn't find a space to put down his china, so he took it back into the kitchen and replaced it on the cleared table. The photograph was no longer there. Upstairs he could hear Julia talking to the man and the woman. He stood undecided at the sink and looked again into the garden, to where the group had lain in the grass. After a moment he went up the narrow stairs. The man was holding a gun in the crook of his arm.

'I see you shoot, old chap,' said the man.

'Not really,' Claude said. 'At one time my eldest son and I had a target up in the garden, but I rarely bother now.'

'Bit different from the weapons we had in the war, eh?' observed the man.

Claude didn't answer. He held his hand out and took the gun and went to the window.

'Oh, Claude, not now, darling,' said Julia. 'You'll wake the baby.'

'It's all right, girl, it's not loaded.' Pushing wide the window, he pressed the gun to his shoulder and looked along the line of the barrel at a patch of grass, the rusted frame of a child's tricycle and a statue without a head. He took aim and pulled the trigger, firing an imaginary pellet at the statue.

'It's quite well made,' he told the man, straightening up and placing the gun on the piano top, carefully, so as not to dislodge any of the numerous ornaments. 'It's remarkably accurate for its type.'

'But hardly capable of killing?' asked the man, uneasily.

'No,' said Claude, and shut the window. He sat down on the sofa beside the woman. She was now wearing spectacles, studying the photograph.

'Who's that?' she asked, pointing at the figure on the left of the picture. Whoever he was, he seemed a little isolated from the others and his face was indistinct.

'That was Edward,' said Julia. 'He was awfully nice. Quiet, but very nice.'

'Awfully quiet and awfully nice,' echoed Claude.

'And who's that?' asked the woman. 'That person on the bench?'

'That's Shebah,' said Julia. 'A friend of Lily's. It's a very typical pose. She won't tell anyone how old she is and she's devoted to Lily, though they fight all the time.'

The woman looked at the girl who had been pregnant. She wasn't very much to look at with that beaked nose and her untidy hair. She wondered how long and in what way Claude had known her and whether he had often sat with his arm about her shoulders. Had he met her perhaps when she'd come to the shop to buy something? Probably not. She didn't look the kind of person who could afford to buy anything.

'And that one's Norman,' said Julia. 'Everyone calls him Victorian Norman because he wears round high collars, and Lily says he's Victorian. I don't know why really. He works in a factory and he once lived in a room above Lily. He's self-educated. He doesn't like to say how old he is either.'

She bent her head and peered at the celluloid image of Victorian Norman. It was him – and yet it wasn't him at all, she decided. He was dressed as he should be with the high collar framing his face, and his Chelsea boots were just visible in the grass, but in the end it was only a photograph and lifeless. She bent closer and imagined that his nostrils were flaring slightly, that he was about to laugh in that manner peculiar to him . . .

control which made it impossible to break with my undesirable friends. I would in the end survive. There might even be more opportunities open to me now, were I to return to conformity. To give expression to my affection for Lily I appear to be 'one of them'. I have only gradually come to understand the difference between myself and these others. They have broken the tape of environment emotionally, whereas I have done it mentally. Which leaves me free to return to harbour whenever I choose. Lily left home very early, in a wild stampede of open revolt, splintering in the process the whole framework of her background, so that now she is sad to find that she has nothing to return to but ruins. I spent ten years preparing my family for my departure. At thirty I at last lifted the brass knocker of the house in Morpeth Street. When I entered and put my corporeal body fair and square into the dark interior of the now familiar hall, I shivered with delight. It was the shiver of the natural swimmer who until this moment had not known the exact location of the river. With Lily gone, nothing has altered – save that she has gone. When I think of her, which I do some part of every day, it is with seriousness. There have been so many words we have spoken to each other. In one day I almost see her a dozen times in the street. Sometimes it is the line of her jaw, sometimes a lank length of hair lying across the velvet collar of a coat. I am always surprised at what I feel when I actually come face to face with her. For one thing there are brown stains on her teeth from too much smoking, and for another I had forgotten how parched are her lips. Her whole mouth puckers with dryness. When she looks at me, which she did just a moment ago, not smiling but with intensity, I want to laugh. I can feel my mouth begin to tremble at the edges. She is trying to tell me that I alone understand, which I don't, and even if I did, the effect is somewhat spoiled by my having watched her look just as intensely at almost everyone. She has indiscriminate intensity of manner. Also, I am disillusioned by her to an extent that I find remarkable, as I did not intend to have illusions. When in the beginning she called me her rock of ages, I did not suppose I would become a rock. When she constantly referred to my qualities of steadfastness and my integrity, I did not comprehend that it was her feminine way of obscuring the fact that she felt no desire for me. The advantages have only slightly outweighed the frustrations. It has meant I could watch her undress for bed, that I could soap her back, her faintly sallow back curved over the plastic bowl in the sink, and that I could keep track of her numerous attachments. On occasions I could be her petal, her gold flower, her dulce boy, her jewel. Lulled by her glucose endearments, my fingers, slippery with soap, would begin a shy glissade over the surface of her damp and bony ribs, only to find that in a moment the golden boy, the petal boy, would be banished utterly and the man of rock be called upon. Towel draped about her chest for protection, she would extol my many virtues, rubbing herself dry the while, edging sideways and with decorum into the all-enveloping folds of her cherry dressing-gown, leaving me alone at the sink with outstretched hands still damp with soap, outmanoeuvred to the last. It's true, of course, that I am Lily's very own personal rock, that I can behave as spinelessly as I like with other women, without damaging our relationship. It's true also that Lily herself chooses endlessly and unerringly to become involved with men who lack totally those steadfast qualities she so admires in me. At the moment the thoughtful Edward, sitting on the grass with shoulders hunched, looks the exception to the rule, but then he hasn't known Lily very long and the foundations of his character have not yet been exposed to her full and merciless attentions. It's to be hoped that the little frown between his brows is caused by the glare of the sunlight, or the smoke from his cigarette, and not by any uneasiness he may be feeling due to the frequent disappearances of Lily throughout the long night. I could lean forward and whisper my congratulations in his ear, if only to enjoy the astonishment blossoming on his pleasant face. It is not given to us all to achieve fatherhood so quickly or so effortlessly. And if Lily's choice was made in haste, at least he was chosen. If he is an honourable man there may even be a wedding. Shebah can be both bridesmaid and godmother, and Claude will be best man. The sun will shine and Lily will hold flowers against her bulging waistline, and with any luck I shall be left alone with the gentle Julia.

The tragedy of Claude and Lily lies in the regularity of their nonconformity. Everything being permissible, they are lost to the delights of the unpermitted. Julia and I, not being so emancipated, can appreciate to the full the bittersweet flavour of infidelity. In the brief seclusion of the bathroom last night she struggled rapturously to remove my hands from the buttons of her blouse. From her armpits came the seed-cake smell of the virtuous female.

Though I do not believe in God, despising with true party fervour the opiate of the people, I am wrapped tight in childhood bands of Sunday school faith. That I am mortal – meaning that I am doomed to die – does not, as it does for Shebah, cause me to be in mourning for my life. When I climb mountains I am intensely aware of my healthy body breathing air purified by height, and were I to receive some warning of impending death I would most certainly lift up mine eyes to the hills. Though as a Marxist I would be conscious of the puerile sentiments of my dying mind, as a sensualist I could only sink down on my knees with heartfelt praise. The little things that hold me close to the centre of my own universe fling Lily into the void. I have no illusions as to my usefulness in the social scheme of things. That I work for a fair wage does not mean that privately I contribute constructively to anything but my own shadow. I more than accept the realisation of my own unreality, whereas Claude and Lily and the biologically tormented Shebah wrestle day long, life long, in a ludicrous attempt to tear the stars from the sky and bring them within reach of their destructive fingers. That they never succeed only darkens their blood and does any amount of damage to their overloaded brains. It would not surprise me if Lily died of an explosion in the head, eyes charred in their sockets, features contorted with agony. I shall merely fall into a profound sleep, and only a pocket mirror held to my lips will show that my lungs have ceased to function. Likewise my little Julia. Last night I received nothing and everything from her inhibited being. That is to say, I was given in abundance the sweet smell of her hair and skin, the trusting proximity of her body, the dulcimer tones of her ladylike voice.

Shebah being here this weekend has partially spoiled my enjoyment. In the confines of the kitchen in Morpeth Street she was sufficiently restricted to be cautious. Her discretion guaranteed that she remain once weekly in her wickerwork chair by the cupboard. But the air here, and the trees and the flowers, not to mention the pride-swelling injury to her leg, may well unhinge her. Accustomed as she has been all these years to perpetual vistas of chimneys black with soot and a day-by-day denial of her existence by a hostile world, she could not be blamed for growing lyrical about this experience. It is not often one spends a weekend in the country. If she so far forgets herself as to let slip some echo of this visit to my girl-friend when next they meet, how shall I counteract her words? I find that the business of lying is exhausting and robs the deceit of its bloom. Lily has no such difficulty. She would hardly recognise the truth if it hit her in the face. She will tell Edward, if she has not already done so, that Claude's rifle fire this morning was meant for him. 'Because you see, Edward,' she will tell him, not for a moment allowing him to be torn from the eloquence of her eyes, 'he loves me, he always has.' I must admit I am curious to know for whom the shot was intended. I cannot believe that Claude is an inferior marksman. Therefore I cannot believe that he aimed at Shebah. Perhaps he fired at me, angry at my evening-long attention to his mistress. Perhaps the sane and loyal Julia, seeing him bulky in the open window of the upstairs room, flew like a bird while his finger already whitened on the trigger, and jerked his elbow outward. The reality of the shot is established, though the identity of the victim is unknown. I cannot believe that Claude cares enough about Shebah to wound her. Only Shebah and Lily care that much about Shebah. Lily thinks Shebah unique and magnificent in her arrogance. If I am Lily's golden boy, her petal boy, then Shebah is her diamond brain. Shebah's magnificence Lily attributes to her temperament and her race. I ascribe it to the absence of her ovaries. An insistently expressed egotism is the keynote of the hypogonad character. Coupled with, and dependent upon, this is an active resentment towards a world that is inadequately mindful of imagined excellence. Give Shebah back her ovaries and Lily would cease to find her interesting. As to Shebah's arrogance being in any way racial, in all history only the Jews went so passively to the slaughter.

Between Lily and Shebah lies distance measured in years. Between Lily and me there is a distance which is due to the difference in our sex. There are, of course, other kinds of distance that are calculable. There is a distance between people that is measurable, caused by the class system. The sun is about ninety-three million miles away mathematically. Visually it is just behind that tree and a little below that cloud. Lily is much nearer and Shebah is so close that I can feel her bare toe protruding from her openwork sandal, irritably jigging up and down against my shoulder blade. She would probably like to give me a strong kick in the back of the neck, just where it joins my spinal column, and pitch me forward on to my nose, but then she has to pretend that she is weak from loss of blood. Not that she bled at all, or if she did it was an internal bleeding and not for the eye to see. Consequently I cannot give her the sympathy that may be justly hers. Everything depends on other factors. For instance I am only sprawled here on the grass in all this heat because it is summer. It is a seasonal sprawling. Also, if it were not Whitsun or Bank Holiday or whatever it is, I would be at the factory. And if I were not Lily's best friend I should not have been invited to spend the weekend at Claude's, he being Lily's best friend. We are all best friends and it is not a limited company. Across Claude's face continually flits the expression of a man in search of God. 'I cannot give you the whole,' he says, 'I can only give you a part.' He blended perfectly into the purple sofa in Lily's living-room in Morpeth Street. The candle dripped wax on to the brick hearth and garlands of coloured paper, put up for Christmas and long since forgotten, criss-crossed in loops of orange and blue above his saintly head. His head was saintly merely in its appearance. He constantly told Lily she ought to cleave to him and become one. Once he woke in the middle of the night, in spite of his double dose of sleep-inducing pills, and pissed into the Victorian chamber pot that stood on a small table beside the brass bed. The pot being full of dried earth, hard as rock, could not absorb his offering, and the liquid spilled on to the wooden floor, waking Lily, who in the light of the still-burning candles saw him on tiptoe, bunching himself in his two hands, the shadow of his body huge across the fireplace wall, a drunken dancer tripping the light fantastic. The chamber pot belonged originally to Billie, the Wild Colonial Boy. The removal men, responsible for the safe conduct of Lily's effects when she left Morpeth Street, dropped the pot as they descended the grey stone steps. The fall cracked the chamber neatly into two halves and dislodged the lump of earth. They swept the halves of china into a refuse bin, but the clod lay for two days on the pavement. I did hope a shower of rain might miraculously revive it, but the twig stayed dead and crumbled into dust. 'How sad,' said Lily, when I told her. Set all round this courtyard, in Grecian urns and tubs bound with copper, Claude has grown a multitude of plants whose names I do not begin to know. Claude himself hardly knew a few months ago, before his fervour for the soil began.

'You know where you are, cocker,' he informed me last night, 'when you plant a seed.'

Now there, he and Edward should have room for discussion.

Julia, every morning, draped in a dressing-gown of grenadine silk, waters each pot with deliberate care. Had I so far forgotten myself this weekend as to return the compliment and urinate into one of the stone urns bedecked with blossom, Claude would doubtless have shot me along with Shebah. His eyes continually widen in their search for decay that may suddenly appear upon his precious leaves. The plants themselves give off a purely chemical aroma, besprayed as they are from dawn till dusk with insecticide.

Last night the head gardener in his bathrobe of many colours spent some time with his spray, having made sure beforehand that in his absence I would not employ my time pursuing Julia. It meant that I spent a restless night on the couch with the dog for company, while Claude refreshed by his night-air administrations, noisily attended to his other flower, his gentle budlet released from her glass spectacles, her buttoned blouse, lying amid the lavender sheets of the ornate bed. It is only of small comfort to imagine that perhaps she thought of me while undergoing her Claudian atrocities. Twice Julia came to Morpeth Street. Once in spring and again in winter. In the spring Claude had cut her hair and she wore a cream-coloured skirt that she washed without fail every one of the three nights of their stay. In winter she had a cold that tinged her nostrils pink and she wore her hair in a bun at the nape of her neck. The sight of her white neck caused Lily to scrub her own neck for several nights afterwards with a toothbrush, in an attempt to remove some of the ingrained dirt.

'Did you see it?' she asked me unnecessarily. 'Like milk, Norman. Honest to God, like a glass of milk.'

When this weekend I saw the dapper tiles and shining taps in Claude's bathroom it became abundantly clear why Julia has such a neck. The bathroom in Morpeth Street held no usable bath. A copper geyser sagged outwards like a disused tea-urn, and a faint smell of gas hung forever in the air. Less privileged guests slept on a divan beside the bath and emerged the next morning partially poisoned by fumes. I myself went home on a Tuesday, and still do, to bathe. Lily had to make do at the sink.

Looking at Lily now she does not appear to be unhappy, but then it is not at all apparent that she has any capacity for happiness. When she falls into my arms my laugh becomes a spasm.

She frequently tells me that my sound for laughing is absurd. My laugh is, in its way, like the length of my hair, a deliberate eccentricity. It is not so much a sign of comical relaxation as a method of releasing excitement. Thus, when the shop bell rang yesterday morning, and Claude with weary eyes held out his arms to enfold Lily, I laughed with elation, sensing the coming confusion. Only the voice of Shebah, raised in extreme complaint as her foot was crushed, invaded their intimacy. The temperature of the shop rose slightly with our entrance. A flush suffused Julia's rounded cheeks.

Lily has told me often about the house, about the pictures, the harp, and the beds of French design. But I had not comprehended what it would be like visually until I saw it for myself. Shebah, her face struggling to preserve its tragic mask, let fall her bags upon the sofa. That Edward failed to share our excitement was to be expected. For him, the upstairs room, packed like a bazaar, was only another room and not a plateau of historical importance. Here, Claude had unfurled his flags of domestic war, begat his numerous children – there on the rug before the open hearth, in winter and in summer. Here, the immortal Billie had spoken to Lily for the last time. Claude, hitherto the chief clown in his frock coat of Indian origin, worn on his circus visits to Morpeth Street, now came into his element, out of the sawdust ring and into the glittering arena of antiquity, the dealer in furniture, the man of property. He wagged his bearded head with pleasure at our appreciation. He informed us that the kettle was on to make tea and that we really must see his roses.

'Well, Shebah,' he said. It was not a question, only a greeting. All the time Claude did not really take his attention away from Edward, standing placidly beside the piano. He watched

Edward's hand search for his cigarettes and only when he had lit one and begun to inhale did he move forward to offer one of his own.

'No, no, thank you,' said Edward. He fumbled in his pocket. 'Have one of mine.'

'No, old boy, I prefer these,' Claude said. Through an open door in another room I heard Julia tell Lily how well she was looking. Julia was mistaken, though not insincere. When I saw Lily at the station I too thought she looked well. Only on the bus journey did I begin to observe, like a picture coming into focus, the signs of exhaustion on her face. It is possible that she has never looked healthy, that her febrile features are a matter of inheritance.

It is hard to tell how Edward sees Lily. Being a geologist it may be that he will not commit himself until he has dug a little deeper. Last night he became assertive. Boyishly he laid a nicotine-stained hand across Lily's grateful shoulders. Shebah, clutching her spotted handkerchief, the receptacle for her frequent and ecstatic tears, played to the full her role of purity, the spiritual being among the crowd of debauchees.

'I think you're all terrible, darlings,' she cried, rolling her eyes like a stag at bay.

'I reckon,' said Claude, 'that we're more to be pitied than envied.'

'Pitied?' Shebah almost choked with indignation. 'Pitied, with you all getting what you bloody well want?'

'I reckon we never get what we want,' said Claude. 'None of us ever has.'

Edward looked quickly at Lily and away again.

'Oh, I don't know, darling,' said Lily. 'Life's not so bad.' With a belly-ful of trouble she tried to minimise the implication in

Claude's remark. 'We do have a lot of fun.' She laughed and leaned her head against Edward's shoulder. 'I should have worn my hat,' she murmured, 'the one I wore at my father's funeral. You remember the night Liz got attacked in the street and there was a fog and no one could go home . . . ' She lapsed into silence. Either she felt genuine sorrow at the thought of her dead daddy or she didn't want Edward to know about the bedding arrangements that particular night.

'Oh darling,' said Shebah, 'I remember so well. Your poor dead father.' Unable to resist the opportunity afforded for criticism she said: 'Miss Evans stayed downstairs. She slept in the brass bed, didn't she? I seemed to be required to rest on the couch. Not that I got any sleep with you singing away in the kitchen, as if you'd come from a wedding. Such an odd way of expressing respect for the departed.' She smiled wildly, as if to take the sting out of her words. Strangely, of us all, her face alone bears the stamp of depravity. The exodus of Edward and his birthday mate caused her to grimace as if in pain. Claude, knowing full well the havoc it would wreak upon her temperamental nervous system, quietly refilled her glass. His eyes were beamy with mischief. Despite this he managed to be aware that, under the table, my hand caressed the linen-covered thigh of his Julia. His professional eye lit up at contact with a situation not entirely distasteful to him. Secure in his knowledge of me, he raised the gloomy Shebah to her sandalled feet and led her away. Julia made a great show of washing the dishes. Shebah asked to be allowed to assist with the washing up. She had no intention of doing so, she merely wished to let me know once and for all that I was a libertine. As she climbed the stairs her voice was heavy with annoyance, her vowels laden with feeling. A showy sigh preceded each step of the way.

Hot steam had misted Julia's glasses. Under my arm her narrow shoulders were stooped. I removed her spectacles and, like a bird with its beak open for food, almost blind, she protested ... 'Don't, Norman' ... and in the middle of her protest I kissed her mouth. When I had wiped her glasses clean I replaced them on the bridge of her polished nose. Her hand came up to settle them more firmly, leaving a smear of soap across her cheek. It is in little things that I find extremes of excitement: the erotica of the wholly ordinary explored to their furthest limits. I found a ravishment of sensation in the near-sighted blinking of her eyes. When I had taken off her apron, I put my pinnyless little Julia on my lap and we talked. The conversation was, as usual, about Lily, safely tucked away in the guest-room, making a father out of the unsuspecting Edward. During these last three years I have been endlessly involved in discussions about Lily – her past, her present, her unpredictable future.

'What if Edward thinks it's a bit strange – her being pregnant so quickly? What if he doesn't want to marry her?' Julia was genuinely concerned. Her mouth quivered with compassion. 'What if the baby looks like Billie?'

Claude has taught her nothing, it seems, which is in part her charm. Lily and I have already talked about the possibility of a Billie baby, and found it amusing. To console Julia I drew her closer to me. I was happy enough to be content with stroking her hand. With Julia I find my delights belong to the primary school – my first Best Friend, 'Please sit by me, you can drink my milk if you like' – a moist flash of emotion, a lisping turn of phrase, an adorable secret to be whispered into an adorable ear. The realisation that to Claude she is a big grown-up girl only accentuates my pleasure.

Safe in my arms she snuggled against me, able to be confiding. 'I envy Lily, you know,' she told me. 'I do really, Norman. Yes, honestly I do.' Her breath smelled warm and smoky. Upstairs Shebah's laugh stuttered out, like a stick dragged at speed across railings, and terminated abruptly.

'You are so understanding, Norman,' Julia told me. 'You are so nice.'

Nicely I squeezed her waist in appreciation. After a while because the unseen Claude in the room above was not conducive to relaxation, I suggested we go into the garden. Never wasteful of time, Julia took a bucket from under the sink and filled it at the tap, in preparation for watering Claude's roses. In mild jealousy I sat at the garden table and watched her attend to his plants. Shebah's shadow, in time to music, crossed the yard. The gramophone was probably driving her to a pitch of distraction. Her face this morning, when she was shot, drooped in an hilarious parody of pain. I do not doubt that she was shocked, but I could not help laughing. When I used to take her home at night from Morpeth Street, she would often fling her arm across her eyes and lean against the pillars of some house. Her catatonic pose would be held until, sensing that I was becoming impatient, she would let loose a funereal groan. Having heard her cry wolf so often and so loudly, I am no longer able to make the appropriate sounds of sympathy. I do understand her predicament – to be always missing the crucifixion she craves, to be allied but isolated from a race that has suffered, to wait for ever for a Messiah who will never come! That is why Claude's action this morning could be interpreted as an act of charity. Shebah herself might have preferred a near death attack with attendant blood transfusions and bunches of grapes, but then beggars cannot choose. Hearing her voice from where I sat in the shadowy garden last night, raised high in complaint and demented laughter, one would have thought she was intent on butchering Claude. Julia, watering the roses, glanced at the open window. 'She sounds so cross,' she said.

In mock protection I rose and put my arm about her waist. She was too kind to draw away from me abruptly – and besides, the wine, drunk in large quantities throughout the evening, was having a liberating effect upon her.

There were two things jostling in my mind. Whether it were nobler to suffer the slings and arrows of an outraged Claude or to be content with a gentle embracing beyond the yard and in the long grass of the little perfumed garden. I have found with women that nothing is predictable. The most natural-seeming conquest can turn a woman into a virago of puritanism, and the shyest woman can suddenly become a changeling of delicious eagerness. The worry was where to conduct my exploratory advances with some semblance of dignity. Claude's particular form of humour would delight in catching me beneath some tree in a crucial state of undress. Had I known last night about his predilection for firing guns into the undergrowth, I should never have debated. In the end it was Julia who solved the problem by suggesting innocently that she show me the barn, which lay at right angles to the house, and contained Claude's larger treasures. To the accompaniment of shouts and groans from Shebah on her couch in the room above the shop, Julia unlocked the wooden door and switched on the light. The place was filled with tables, chairs, sofas and cabinets, clear to the end of the barn. It is a pity I have not been able to tell Lily about last night, the situation being so dramatic: a film set, a dream fantasy concocted by Claude, ever the ideal host, with sofas and divans on every side of me and my little Julia stepping ahead of me.

At the far end of the barn I made the beautiful discovery that the building was L-shaped, that there was a little avenue of sofas on our left, almost in darkness. In particular there was one sofa upholstered in green velvet with a gilt curved back and a seat as wide as a small divan. I sat down on it hardly able to breathe. Julia was busily examining a small table, presumably for signs of woodworm, peering at its surface with disproportionate interest. 'Oh look, Norman,' she said with gentle dismay, 'a little mark – just here – and look, another one.' Eyebrows raised in alarm she stroked the damaged wood. Afraid that her concern would make her fetch Claude, I left my sofa and inspected the table, though I couldn't see anything, but at least I had my arm round her waist. I kept remembering what Lily has told me on various occasions – that a woman will always know when she is about to be molested, and even if she doesn't like you she will have difficulty in breathing, though the cause must not be confused with passion. I could not really tell whether Julia was breathing normally or not, because I could hear nothing above the thudding of my own heart, so Lily's advice was in itself of little use. I did know Julia liked me, and remembering how little time there was then as now, or ever, I pulled her round to face me and kissed her. I don't think she was very responsive, but a middle-class upbringing is a great help. If you have been taught that a refusal will cause offence and that politeness is next to godliness, then you don't push a house guest away in a hurry. At least Julia didn't and somehow, with a great deal of loud exhalation on my part and a variety of kittenish mewings from her, I contrived to reach my goal, my green savannah, my velvet sofa in the gloom, and place her upon it. I had to keep her on it by sheer force, not by my arms exactly but rather by a strong pressure of my mouth against hers, which was more painful than exciting, but at least it was something. The wine had made me lightheaded and we both seemed to be trapped under glass and I couldn't hear a thing save for the muffled drum beat in my ears. Suddenly she stopped resisting and lay more or less inert beneath me. I cannot say she was willing. More likely, as Lily would no doubt tell me, it was only that she had decided to get it over with as quickly as possible. She lay with her eyes closed tight, spectacles awry on the bridge of her sharp little nose. I kept my eyes on her face all the time I removed my clothes. I can undress more rapidly than most. I don't even leave my socks on. I didn't care about Julia being fully clothed if she preferred it, but I wanted nothing between me and the cool surfaces of her little protesting hands except my skin, goose-pimpling in the chill air. As I straightened up, bare to the elements, ready to spring upon my hostess, pausing only a moment to stretch the toe of my right foot, numb from the constriction of a Chelsea boot, I saw a little window half-obscured by creeper that I had not seen before. Outside the glass, blurred only fractionally, I glimpsed the sardonic face of Claude. Shock momentarily paralysed me. Only my big toe, crushed yellow like a flower left between the pages of a book, jiggled in an attempt to restore circulation. Then my reflexes saved me and jerkily, like an old film running backwards, I dressed again. I could not really see the smile on Claude's features, but knowing him I could imagine it. When Julia opened her eyes I was fixing my tie. Puzzled but infinitely relieved, she raised herself from the sofa and resumed her inspection of the worm-afflicted table. If she felt any confusion she showed no sign of it and one hand domestically secured the few remaining clips of her hair.

'Norman,' she said after only a moment, 'I do think I should tell Claude about this table.'

I could only agree, and we walked back along the narrow strip of barn. Claude was waiting for us. He was standing by his roses, not touching them, just watching the slight movement of the leaves as they bounced gently in the night breeze. I do wonder if he'd have continued to spy through the small window had I not seen him. Knowing Claude, it is possible. The thought is an erotic one, even more stimulating than the taking of the submissive Julia. As we went into the house Claude laid his arm across my shoulders and squeezed my upper arm with his stubby fingers.

Shebah was sitting in the living-room, the two dogs at her feet, her hands folded on her lap. She gave me a look of hatred and then one of sweet reproach.

Claude poured us all another drink and then suggested that we should sing 'Happy Birthday' to Lily and Edward. I almost felt that with his attention to detail he would show us a hole in the wall through which we might watch silently or otherwise the celebrating communicants within the bedroom. But all we did was to stand bunched outside the latched door and sing our greetings.

Inside, Lily gave a ho-ho-ho of polite laughter. She is constantly trying to please, to win approval, to make amends. This I understand only because she has tried, in part, to explain it to me. She has gone to bed with numerous strangers rather than offend. Claude did attempt to enter the room, but Julia restrained him. Shebah, surprisingly, was trembling. The bracelets on her plump arms slithered with agitation. Still singing, we returned to the living-room to resume our positions. Julia sat in the large armchair and crossed her legs. Her hand came down to straighten her dress, but she caught me looking at her and rubbed her knee instead. The titillation afforded at the thought of Lily and Edward wantonly together in the guest-room, coupled with her little adventure in the barn, so inconclusive to me, had made her coquettish. The warm breeze from the open window blew across her hair. She patted her head with a capable hand and touched her flushed cheeks. We were all, for various reasons, or perhaps the same reason, in a state of elation. It was not only the drink, because we had consumed enough by now to put us all in a melancholy stupor. Shebah, posturing sternly, placed a grubby finger to her mouth and studied the oil painting above the fireplace. Her pig-tailed head turned from side to side in near blind examination. Performing a few steps of what may have been a minuet, she tripped about the glittering room. As if better to observe her, I slid to the floor and leaned against Julia's knees.

Absorbed in a vision of herself that was wholly music-hall in origin, the red fingers scrabbling to lift her tight skirt higher, Shebah cavorted with corybantic fervour. Claude weaved his way down the room, arms held out like a wrestler, to fetch another bottle from the cupboard. Shebah misunderstood his mission for a moment and imagined he wished to partner her. At his avoidance, she scowled. Lily, had she been present, would have murmured how sad it all was.

I felt comfortably at ease. Not for me the complicated subtleties of atmosphere that constantly assail Lily. For myself, I prefer to see things as they appear to be, reality being stimulating enough for my needs. When Lily has drunk too much she turns with an 'O Christ!' of longing to whoever is nearest. The intensity of her desire to be liked causes her to weep upon unlikely shoulders. I do hope she conducted herself last night with sensibility as she lay in Edward's arms. The success of her plan to make him a legal, if not natural, father of her child depends on her avoidance of indulging in the truth.

When I marry my girl-friend Jean, I shall be happy enough. Though politically I do not recognise class, my inner man rejoices at the limitations that such a system imposes: to be respectable and yet roam at will beyond the barrier. To live wholly in Lily's world would in the end defeat my aims. I derive enormous satisfaction from being a wolf in sheep's clothing. Bless the squire and his relations, keep us in our proper stations.

Up to a point, last night my proper station would have been at the feet of Julia but for the talkative and restless Shebah. Having sung her song of divine forgiveness several times, she sank into a high-backed chair almost in the centre of the room. Her feet stuck straight in front of her, she was completely hidden. Only one hand hung down over the arm of the chair. To Claude, facing her in a cane chair at the end of the room, she must have looked like Napoleon in exile, brooding over past victories. For me, behind her, she was a Zuleika of the river, trailing her scarlet fingers listlessly across the carpet, alone in a punt pulled by the current.

'What's up, old girl?' I shouted, kicking the back of her chair with my foot.

She didn't reply, merely snarled. My mouth was conveniently close to Julia's ankle. I licked her skin. She fidgeted but was frightened of moving her foot too brutally in case she kick out my teeth. Taking advantage of her dilemma, I caressed the plump calf of her leg and dug my fingers into the damp bend of her knees. The pleasure I gained from pestering her in such a way was exquisite. Two little hands protestingly caught at my head and shook me.

'Don't,' she breathed. 'Please don't, Norman dear.'

She was worried about Claude, but I was not. Having allowed me to stand naked and unadorned in his barn with his mistress, I felt it would have been surprising if he had suddenly objected to my chaste handling of her limbs.

'I do wish you wouldn't,' she whispered.

'Come downstairs with me,' I urged.

'No, I can't, really I can't.'

'Yes, you can. Come downstairs.'

'Norman dear, please don't. Claude will see you.'

With a sudden and delightful show of indignation she disengaged her foot and moved away from me. Lying on the floor, I saw only her sensible shoes and her shapely legs. I almost, briefly, felt like one of those men who wear aprons and pay women to walk all over their tortured bodies. Then I suddenly imagined myself very tall, which is wishful thinking as I am extremely small, though in proportion. I cannot remember feeling tall before. Maybe it was a glimpse of Julia's feet going from me – that and the thought of those perverts of the apron world, giving me a false feeling of superiority and nobility.

After a time the denseness of the carpet on which I lay affected my nasal passages. When I opened my eyes the room spun like a top. I heard Claude saying 'You are so wise, my dear, you accept it all.' With that I jumped to my feet. I saw the back of Shebah's head and Claude staring up at her face as if she were his dearly beloved, and before he could notice me I went down the stairs. I did hope Julia might be standing by the sink filling the kettle, but she wasn't. I watered the geranium on the sill and looked for bread in the cupboard. On the wall, above the empty hamster's cage, was a drawing done by Lily in the days when she first met Claude. It was of herself, of course, staring out forever in the role of the child-woman, endlessly gazing with sensitivity at nothing in particular. I feel it would give Lily consummate relief to say that she did not care about that one living there or that one dying there, and meaning it; just to move away without turning round finally to wave to those she says she loves. The unbearable sadness of her supposed world, her private globe, in which she lies impossibly mangled by unending imagined conflicts, turns her like a fish in a pool.

I found a pen in the knife drawer and underneath the drawing I wrote: 'This is a picture of a pregnant girl.' Then I put the date. I stood in the outer shop and visualised Billie edging his way between the tables and ornaments. Part of him must have been agreeably buoyant at coming to such an individualistic place. When he was here he purchased a stuffed mallard for thirty shillings and told Claude to keep the change. According to Claude, who may have been speaking less than the truth, he dropped it, case and all, in the yard when getting into his motor car. He left the glass all over the concrete. Claude, to be even, directed him a good ten miles out of his route north, and kicked the glass into the flower beds, before taking Lily out for a healing walk.

'She howled like a dog at each tree,' he told me.

'I was utterly mute all the way,' Lily told me.

Between the two it is safe to say that Lily experienced a form of suffering. I am not sure what to think about her continual love pains. It is like when I try to explain what it means to me to climb mountains, hills though they be. My explanation is deliberately evasive because I do not intend anyone to understand, though I do offer such items as the air, the view, the combined play of muscles when climbing. I never refer to my mountains as female, nor do I betray myself by the use of the possessive pronoun. When Lily describes her pain, her sadness, her desolation, she shows no such reticence. In the end she talks of abstractions. That is why, when she attempted to kill herself, I experienced a shock out of all proportion to the deed. That she might do so was predictable, that she nearly accomplished it was incredible. There seemed to be a purity of intention that I had not comprehended in her.

I looked at the drawing again and then went upstairs. Shebah was shouting at Claude. I slipped through the room unseen and went into the bathroom where, washing her hands with lilac-scented soap, stood Julia.

'I wondered where you were,' she said.

Her tone was friendly. Possibly she felt I could not commit an offence in a bathroom. As it happened I was no longer intending to do so. I was content to sit on the edge of the bath and have a conversation with her. Women will do strange things out of gratitude. They will even confide why they will not be seduced, forgetting that they pretended they had not understood the intention.

'Do you think, Norman,' asked Julia, 'that Claude looks better?'

She gazed at herself short-sightedly in the mirror above the hand basin.

'Oh yes, definitely. You've done wonders for him,' I said.

It was after all the truth. She had hidden his bottles of whisky and given him raw eggs to swallow. She had cleaned his living quarters and put the two hundred empty packets of cigarettes into the bin and listened to the nocturnal words mumbled in recurring nightmares. Lily tried to describe what it was he had gone through, but I found it ridiculous and irritating. It had to do with hoof-beats thundering along the corridors of the brain, and an epiphany of someone, less than divine, rising monstrously in the mind, intent on destruction.

I took this to mean that Claude was miserable because his wife had left him and was feeling guilty because he was to blame. I detest both obscurity and self-examination. I suspect these grief-stricken extroverts who tell their innermost thoughts to strangers on buses. Of course it was Lily who told me this, not Claude, and she's not a stranger, and I don't think either of them would talk to a fellow bus traveller. Shebah is perfectly capable of doing so – and in fact indulges quite frequently. It's the gusto with which they analyse themselves so consciously and the self-induced guilt with which they flagellate themselves that annoys me. I do not experience guilt because I am ready to take the consequences of my own actions. I do not find myself in the ludicrous position of having to lay the blame for my illicit sex life at the breast of my mother who may or may not have denied me her nipples. And if the schoolmistress who picked me off the playground asphalt when I was six years old, and massaged the agony of my bruised genitals, was less than wise, then at least I am in the end sensible enough to be grateful to her. Apart from the irritation which does not make negative the overall enjoyment, I derive much pleasure from the detailed confessions of these traumatic blatherers.

'You have no idea how sick Claude was when I first came here,' said Julia. 'Vomiting every hour or so and dopey with pills and quite unable to sit still. Just went round and round like a dog trying to find somewhere to lie down and lick its sores.'

The image was an interesting one. In starched cap Julia followed the shaggy Claude round in ever-decreasing circles until exhausted he fell on to his paws, only to start up again with an animal yelp of pain.

'And it was simply ages before he really slept at night.

Months, you know. He kept seeing a ring she always wore on her finger.'

It is strange how they all fasten on to some article worn by the loved one. Claude and his wife's ring – Lily and the check coat of the Wild Colonial Boy.

'Well, I shouldn't worry now,' I said, looking down at my feet on the cork bath mat. 'He's well on the mend. He looks as if he's thriving.' I was feeling sleepy. My head was like lead. I wanted to go to sleep in the bath and, deep down (it was quite a healthy emotion), I hated Claude. The whole house was littered with enemies of the people, traumatic blood-suckers, indestructible and having all the fun. Lily in bed with Edward – half dead a third of a year ago and now needing to eat enough for two – and Claude at any time about to claim his mate for the night. In fact I like Claude. I always have. There is something about his matter-of-fact insanity that I find refreshing. During the last two years I have become almost an authority, in an amateur way, on eccentrics. And Claude is definitely man-to-man in his approach. One couldn't see him running berserk with a hypodermic syringe, like that doctor from Widnes who, lunging for Lily's thigh, gave her photograph album an injection of behaviour-liberating pethedine. Claude's habit of crushing the bones of the hand when saying good-bye is more jocular than vicious. It will be interesting to note the exact degree of pain registered upon the smooth face of the departing Edward when Claude bids him farewell. I suppose Claude's performance this morning with the air-rifle was a little more than good clean fun, but he did not shoot to kill. Had he mortally wounded Shebah, I wonder where we should have buried the body? The light in the bathroom was very bright. Julia and I were fully exposed and illuminated. Remembering the times Lily has assured me that the reasons for women being unwilling are mainly visual and so obvious as to be generally overlooked by men – the mascara running down the kiss-damp face, the soiled underwear, the cornfield stubble of shaven legs, the stretch lines on the stomach – I stood suddenly upright and jerked the light cord down and released it and us into the obliterating darkness. I was only going to attempt a mild mingling of our mouths, a braille-like roving with my hands. I first removed her glasses and placed them with care on the shelf above the hand basin. I nuzzled her hair with my mouth and mumbled 'Little pet, little dove' into her hair. I had just unbuttoned the first two buttons of her blouse when the light was switched on again. I had not even managed to kiss her. Lily stood with the light cord in her hand, dressed in her cotton nightgown, and behind her Claude, not smiling, looking at the two buttons undone on the blouse of his mistress. He put his arm round Lily and dipped his head into her neck, crooning 'O God, girl', or something like that, as if he really cared. I was for a moment afraid I had overdone it, that this time he was angry, but Lily looked at ease and she is a barometer of atmosphere. In her eyes there was nothing but curiosity. Then the two of them, Claude with lowered head and Julia with a faint agitation of her eyelids, went out of the bathroom and Lily stayed at my back looking at her reflection in the mirror. We didn't speak, because she was absorbed in being understanding and compatible with my mood. I did not have a mood to be compatible with and I would have liked to ask her about Edward, except she might have gone on too long and at too great a length, so I just whistled, 'Devon, Glorious Devon'.

I'm not quite sure how much Lily feels, despite her constant articulation. Sometimes I imagine if I could ask her quickly enough what she was thinking at a particular moment before she had time to marshal the words in force, she might answer 'Nothing': a small, round, flat, air-escaping negative. But I have never been swift enough. The words are all there, pyramid-high and tumbling for exit. The shapes they make build up in her emotional structures.

In the living-room Shebah was still singing. She stared at Lily as if she had newly risen from the dead, mouth wide open on a high note of shrill surprise. I was not feeling very cheerful. Twice in one night I had been cruelly interrupted in my pursuit of Julia. Altogether the sort of evening that, had I been on home ground, I would have terminated by winding up the alarm clock and going upstairs. I felt, however, that something might yet happen, though not in any spectacular sense, in that over-crowded room, so long as Claude still ran round and round cracking his invisible whip. He lit a cigarette for Lily, who sat like a pink Buddha in the huge armchair, and poured more wine for Shebah. It was surprising that Shebah had not long since keeled over unconscious, unless canny to the last she had been decanting the drink into the many pots and vases about the room. Claude began to tell me something '... quite impossible to imagine how much is already there to be released, cocker. We all have our postures, you know. I reckon you've got a pretty solid posture.'

He waggled the bowl of his glass under my nose as if he intended to grind it into splinters up my nostrils. 'The only thing to do, man, is to become part of the cosmic flow. Spin like a dervish and never bother to find out what it's about. At my age there's no time left for conjecture ...'

There was much more, but I was trying to reason out what Claude's exact age was and whether he looked it. I was seeing him twenty years ago in air-force blue, dapper and bonny with beardless chin. 'The fantasy life that goes on,' Claude was saying, 'is simply incredible. A million commuters in bowler hats avidly chasing fat women and Lolitas between the jumping print of their evening newspapers. A million breasty girls utterly unaware that babies must be fed naturally, not handed the bottle every four hours . . . ' His mouth opened and shut as the words buzzed like wasps through his jammy lips. '. . . but *she* was different. Now she was a woman.' Who was he alluding to now? Surely not Lily.

'The Jews are a very *sympatico* race you know, cocker,' he continued, taking me by the arm and not so much leading as pushing me towards his bedroom. His fingers, clamped round my upper arm, were like steel; his voice flowed on endlessly.

'Generations of persecution have given wings to their sensitivity. If you blind the nightingale the song will be sweeter. It is nature. All life is a circle and the end of all our beginnings is to arrive where we started and to know the place for the first time.' He opened the bedroom door and thrust me inside.

Quite so. I did not know the place, nor had I at any time. I looked intently at the elegant bed, the shell-pink walls, the bitter glimpse of Julia's nightdress half-showing beneath a pillow. Claude undid his shoes. His articulation continued, spattered by grunts as he struggled with his socks. 'Nothing you do will in the end appease the monster that lies in wait for you. For every crime there is a punishment. Every hurt given, every lie told, every atom of suffering deposited by you on the surface of another human being will bring its awful reward. Neither money, nor power, nor threats, nor pleadings, will avail you.'

He sank on to the bed, thrusting out his naked feet, and lit a cigarette, puffing at it energetically, brows deeply furrowed. Suddenly, behind a cloud of smoke, he asked abruptly, 'Did Julia seem to like it?'

'Well, yes and no,' I said. 'More polite than anything, I think.'

I watched his big toes paddling in the quilted coverlet and hoped I was hitting the right conversational note. He put his cigarette down on the edge of the bedside table and began to lift his shirt up from the waistband of his trousers. Was he going to bed, or about to perform some naked dance? Was he perhaps trying to show me that he too was adept at removing his clothes with speed? If so, he was less than convincing. He took at least half a minute to get the shirt over his head, and emerged with scarlet face and disordered beard. 'I don't mind,' he said, rising to his feet and drawing in his stomach. 'That is to say, I mind very much – or would if I could. But the heart's died on me, man. I am but a shell that once lay near to the sea. I imagine I hear the sound of it yet, but it's all a dream.'

He looked thoughtfully at his feet and slapped with one hand at his huge diaphragm. The drink had larded him with fat but he was still impressive. His skin was perfectly smooth, without blemishes. 'I am going to attend to my roses,' he informed me, and reached for his dressing-gown that hung behind the door. He seemed undecided what to do once the cord about his waist was tied. He put one arm inside the pouch of his gown and began to pace across the room.

'Of course she's devoted to me . . . ' He paused and rubbed at his hidden armpit. 'She's utterly loyal . . . if it's loyalty one wants?' He gazed at me as if I had a problem.

'I know, I know what you mean,' I said emphatically, nodding my head vigorously like some bidder at an auction sale. I had no idea what he meant but he seemed in need of affirmation.

'Of course I don't believe a word Shebah says,' he went on, striding past me to the window. 'It's all in her mind, and even if it were true it doesn't change things any.' He stared out of the window for a moment. Then he turned and seized me by the lapels of my jacket.

'Now look here, mate,' he shouted, transforming himself into the bully at large. 'Keep your hands off my woman. I won't stand for it, do you hear?' He trembled with indignation, head thrust back like an illustration of an actor in one of Shebah's out-dated theatre books, face registering rage with nobility, mouth firmly closed. Before I had time to respond in any way myself – I was just about to contort my facial muscles into a portrayal of fear with cunning – he released me and said quite calmly, 'Study the humble bee, cocker. The order of their life is beyond belief.'

He adjusted his dressing-gown and went like a Japanese warrior out of the room. I flattened my hair smooth with my hand and eased my jacket back into shape. The way in which clothes hang on a man can be indicative of character. Though not as orderly as the humble bee, I am neat.

When I returned to the living-room it was empty of Claude and Lily and Julia. Only Shebah, enthroned in her papal chair, sat facing the far wall, arm outflung. I sat down behind her and watched her fat wrist, circled with its handcuff bracelets, twist back and forth above the carpet. After a little while, with a great deal of shuffling and groaning, she began to slew the chair round to face me. In spite of her constant references to her delicate state of health she has the strength of a man. As if driving a difficult and outmoded automobile, she manoeuvred to a halt and, breathing heavily, stared at me with passion. The black beret she always wears was askew on her grey head. My affection for her, though not often manifested, is real. She shares my disillusionment with Lily. She has, in a different way from me, been deprived of her just rewards. She was forced to her chagrin to play the buffoon for Lily's Friday night carnivals. While I was kept from physical union, Shebah was frustrated in her attempts at full communication. Echoing Claude's statement, Lily gave a part but never the whole. I began in my mind to dissolve the fat from Shebah's hips and waist, draw back the folds of her ruined face.

If she can be believed, and why not, she has hinted at affairs of frantic love. Whether they were consummated she has not divulged. What outrageous admirer prised wide her thighs and perpetrated love? The gulf between her notion of an affair and mine, is, like the sun from the earth, ninety-three million miles distant – and yet, it appears, it is she who has been consumed by fire.

As her eyes were telling me across the flower-strewn carpet last night, 'What do you know, darling?' As if to underline her contempt for my ignorance of life, she raised one bangled arm and fluttered her fingers. A graceful movement. That is why later, when she stumbled against Claude's china cabinet, shattering the glass a little and jostling the ornaments within, I felt such surprise. She is not clumsy; her gestures, even those of contempt, are always defined.

Presently Julia, ever busy in her protection of Claude's property, came in, and crouching down behind the sofa began to clean the harp which lay on its side. She gave me a little rag dipped in paraffin with which to wipe the strings. Secure in the knowledge that I was doing a useful job, I lay down beside her on the floor. Claude, returned from the garden, sat on the piano stool and closed his eyes. I could hear the voice of Shebah rising and falling, and once I heard Claude say, 'Yes my dear, you may be right', in reply to some comment she had made. Behind the sofa, immersed in my restorative labour, all was peace and calm: a little oasis of shade in the hectic furnished room. In the old days at Morpeth Street we would all by now, have been sickly clinging to our pillows; Lily's pillow at least, if not Claude's, would be damp with tears. Maybe the difference in the atmosphere was created by the sane and tidy Julia. I no longer wanted to caress her, or to anger my host, nor did I particularly want to clean his harp, but I was a guest and my bed was to be the sofa behind which I lay. I was too inhibited by upbringing to retire there and then. So I continued to rub, rub, rub, with my little rag up and down the silver strings, pleasantly aware of the smell of Julia's hair without being disturbed by it, and thought of my girl-friend a little, and then of Lily, and then of myself. The danger of being on intimate terms with Lily lies in the inevitability with which sooner or later, however environmentally opposed to her mode of thinking, one is contaminated sufficiently to start the sickening process of self-analysis. I did indulge in analysis in the days when I lived at home, but then I liked myself more. Though I am not naturally honest, I have been so by chance. I was mainly thinking about the time Lily attempted to die.

The night before, she had gone classically through the motions of betrayed womanhood – a delicate and crumpled crying before an audience of five grouped round the kitchen table, an attention to tea-making, to being hospitable even though the world had disintegrated so dramatically about her ears such a short time before. Carefully she cleaned her teeth, following this with a girl-guide utterance of obscenity. It was difficult to tell whether the expletive was occasioned by her constantly sore gums, or by the traumatic homecoming of Billie. Perhaps it was due to the toffee she insists Billie gave to her, nestling within a jewellery box. I cannot make that part of her story out. She had not yet got at the gin bottle and it's hard to see how she mistook a wrapped sweet for an engagement ring. She said good night as charmingly and emptily as usual, performed the ritualistic round of handshaking that she affected, a habit instilled in her by her dead and homburg-hatted dad, gave her bargee laugh exposing all her large and now cleaned teeth, told me to make sure we were locked up for the night, and went to sleep in the bed of polished brass.

When, the next morning, I telephoned, the predictable Lily should have answered my persistent pronouncing of her name – a slurred tearful reply at most. Her silence, the emphatic drop of the telephone on to the floor, filled me with alarm. Had I not telephoned, Lily would have had the funeral we have so often talked about – all poppy wreaths and strong men reduced to tears, and a tipsy vicar flinging himself into the freshly dug grave uttering cries of lamentation.

I have rationalised her actions in the only way of which I am capable. She would have replied to my voice if she had not drunk most of the contents of a bottle of gin left by Billie. The alcohol had obliterated her very strong sense of social etiquette and liberated her stubbornness – hence her refusal to speak. The gas she was inhaling had affected the muscles of her throat, had paralysed her organs of speech. Lastly, her emotions had led her to a final pitch of absurdity and she had given way utterly to irresponsibility. That love of life she so often elaborates upon had evaporated like ether exposed to the air. Nothing remained of Lily but poison in the bloodstream, gas in the lungs, and an immature mind seeking escape. She has told me she merely wished to sleep soundly for a few hours, but I can't accept the explanation. Knowing her incapacity for drink, she would have been sleeping long before the need to turn the tap of the cooker.

Whereas Lily before this regrettable incident was a creature of light and shade, amusing and enchanting, harmless and without evil, she is now bracketed firmly in my mind as a hopeless neurotic, a feeble member of society, an enemy of the people. Feeling this, I can still love her, but I no longer feel at ease with her. She has crossed the borderline ahead of me. Shebah is only Lily taken to extremes of eccentricity forty years along. Lily's continued hold on her ovaries may in the end help her to survive, but only comparatively. At least she will be spared hair on her upper lip. Without waxing so lyrical as Claude in his assertions that it is a privilege to live, I do feel that we have no right to choose the moment of our death.

It is still my belief that she will one day be the victim of a murderous assault. Once, coming home late to the house in Morpeth Street, I found the front door ajar. The normal conclusion, the obvious one that somebody had not closed it after entering, did not occur to me. I took out my handkerchief and carefully wiped the curve of the brass knocker and the latch itself. In the dark hall I listened before opening the door of Lily's room. I switched on the light. Lily, in the raincoat she sometimes wore as a nightgown, sat up in the bed and stared at me with sleep-laden eyes. She reached for the packet of cigarettes she always kept under the pillow. I told her about the front door, and that I had expected to find her dead, arms held out in supplication, slivers of flesh scraped from her attacker's face wedged in the little fissures of her nails. She understood that my sympathies would naturally lie with her assassin. Just in case, we closed the heavy wooden shutters over the long window, excluding the moon dipping like a toadstool into a glass of aniseed. I even bought a bolt and nailed it on the inside of her door, but mostly she forgot to use it.

I was feeling unexpectedly disturbed, thinking about all this, when I suddenly heard a thud. Julia knelt upright so that her head was above the level of the sofa and she said, in a tone very chill but still lady-like, 'Oh Christ!'

Shebah was huddled against the wall, hands covering her face.

'How's it going, man?' asked Claude – apparently of me, though he did not look in my direction.

'Fine, fine,' I replied, distracted somewhat by the little moans of distress issuing from the cowering Shebah.

She moved suddenly as if propelled by an almighty hand and touched the case of china figures. I thought she was in one of her appreciation-of-beauty moods, a little accentuated by drink, her pigtail sticking straight out under the black beret, her whole body writhing against the cabinet. How often she has begged to be given patience to endure her load, she with the soul made for loveliness. It appeared to me that she had thrown patience aside and was about to seize her rightful portion, and she might have done if Claude hadn't cried out 'Leave it, Shebah', very stern, as if he was addressing the dog, and on that too harsh note of command Julia ran forward and cradled Shebah in her arms. In a spastic fit of lamentation Shebah tossed her head and jerked the spectacles from Julia's nose.

Claude came to inspect the half-cleaned harp and patted me on the shoulder. 'Well done, man,' he said, and rubbed his chest, leaving a smear of grease. Shebah continued to wail and I sank down into my little world inhabited by a harp, a yard of carpet, and a shadow cast by the golden lamp on the piano.

I felt that the evening's entertainment was almost over, that the manly Claude was about to take down the tent. He began collecting wine glasses and bottles, and presently Shebah made a round of weepy good nights. She who had often cried out 'But

Life is Sweet, my children', more because she liked the poetry of it than because she believed in the sentiment, now stumbled on white sandalled feet out of the room, evidently convinced that life was vile. One of her scarves, like Salome's veil, caught on the door and drifted to the floor. Julia brought blankets from the bedroom and made up my bed on the sofa, like the good little woman she is, smoothing my sheets and plumping up my pillow. They left me, Claude with many instructions about switching off the lights and securing the window, and Julia with a sweet smile playing upon her pale lips.

'Sleep well, Norman dear,' she said without malice, patting the flank of the brown dog that lay asleep on the floor.

I took off my clothes and shoes and lay on the sofa.

When I heard the sound of bedsprings jangling in the outer bedroom – Claude's own particular brand of psychological torture, meant especially for me – I rose and went to the china cabinet and eased open the door. Inside there was a white dog with a coloured snout lying on its side, and a little box decorated with flowers which was in two pieces, and a pair of figures which seemed untouched. One was of a girl in dress and bonnet leaning her elbow on a bird-cage stand, fist bunched against her mouth, and one hand held towards me. A little bird perched on her open palm. The companion figure was a pretty man in knee-breeches with a dimpled face. He was supported at the buttocks by a tree trunk twined about with ivy. As far as I could see both figures were intact. I tried dropping them on the floor but they rolled harmlessly on the carpet. The sleeping dog twitched its ears. I took the china figures into the bathroom. Laying a towel across the cork bath mat and taking the precaution of turning the taps of the hand basin full on, I bent down and struck the two figures one against the other. The hand holding the bird broke at the wrist and rolled under the bath. The little man's leg broke into two pieces. I took the spoiled figures and the pieces back into the main room and replaced them on the shelves inside the cabinet. The dog during my absence had climbed on to the sofa and lay with its tail on my pillow. When the lamps were extinguished there was a rind of light outside the closed windows. The springs of Claude's bed trembled in a final cadenza.

This morning Claude brought me a cup of tea. When he opened the windows, birds sang and sunlight glinted on splinters of glass on the carpet. He went downstairs and came back with a brush and swept the floor, a tuft of beard clenched between his teeth. He did not look in the cabinet at all and when he came to fetch my empty cup he smelled of scented soap and toothpaste, and on the surface of his pink and fleshy chest, revealed by his open dressing-gown, there were two marks faintly scored. Scratch marks of fingernails. Not his.

In the bathroom I looked to see if there were any chippings on the floor, but found nothing but dust and a hair grip, belonging presumably to Julia. I put the clip in the pocket of my jacket without any real reason. I'm not in love with Julia. Shebah tried to turn the handle of the locked door and swore and moved away sighing heavily. I cannot imagine that she wanted to wash, only that she wished to pass water. It may be that she urinated with fright when ten minutes later the pellet hit her in the ankle. I do not know why I harbour at times such intense feelings of antagonism towards her and Lily. Though not an ordinary girl, lying there in a patch of sun Lily is still deserving more of compassion than hatred. My ambiguity distresses me, being at the root emotional, and I do not care for emotions. I do not detest my parents for their futile adherence to the conventions, their blind belief in the dignity of human toil, their comical loyalty to the Royal Family. I do, it is true, take some measure of delight in puzzling my workmates at the factory by a deliberate show of eccentricity, but there is no malice intended. I do not, as Lily does, suffer from being related to my mother and father. Should my own father, as hers did, confide to me one teatime, that life was a cheat and a delusion, I would agree with him without identifying myself personally with his statement; nor would I feel the weight of seventy wasted years. I do not expend energy on uselessly worrying about whether I am understood. It is not necessary to be understood in order to live. Believing, as I do, in Marxist ideology and yet actively participating in the survival of capitalism, I am in much the same dilemma as Shebah: the martyr without a cause. I am cut off from fulfilment. But I do not sympathise with Shebah; I recognise that she is dangerous. The kindness she has received from Julia and Lily, following the breakages last night and her wound this morning, have sunk her into a coma of satisfaction, as she sits on her bench, sugary and quiet. Having obtained such a liberal injection of pity she may well demand another and larger dose before long. Fortunately I do not have to travel home on the train with her. Some other luckless traveller will find her swooning across the carriage seats, clutching her leg as if the marrow had run out. Even Claude at lunch time gave her more ham than the rest of us.

'Get that down you, my dear.'

'Oh darling, I couldn't.'

'No arguments. Eat up. Make a new woman of you.'

'Oh darling.'

The new woman opened her mouth and ate all that was on her plate.

*

Lily has been almost silent since breakfast. She has held the hand of the placid Edward as if afraid he might yet make a break for it. He has thrown sticks for the dog and behaved like a gentleman, which perhaps he is. We will have to wait the few long weeks till Lily tells him the glad tidings of his approaching fatherhood. 'Of course I cannot be sure,' she will say, holding her breath to keep her belly flat, 'but it's almost definite.' It is to be hoped that she does not ask Claude what it was he said to Edward when she and Julia were in the bedroom.

Lily and I arranged some time ago that we would meet in the Kardomah in extreme old age to discuss the outcome of our lives. Shebah, long since buried, will achieve resurrection through memories. From her island retreat off the coast of Scotland, Lily, if not grown bald, will shake her white head and lay a wrinkled hand upon my knee.

'Tell me, Norman, do tell me, flower, what went wrong all those years ago, that weekend with Claude?'

Maybe I shall only remember the sunshine in the garden and the strip of bandage round the ankle of Shebah, her comic flag of truce, and the ham we had for lunch lying on a bed of lettuce leaves.

As Baudelaire tells us, *There is nothing that is not misunderstanding*. Claude is determined to take a photograph. The camera, like the gun, points at us all.

5

'Why are they all friends?' asked the woman. 'They're so different. All of them. Lily and Norman and the old woman.' It was extraordinary how familiar they became when she named them like that.

'Yes, they are different,' agreed Julia, 'though they all seem alike when they're together. Claude seemed like them too, when they were together.' She frowned. 'I'm not like them at all.'

'No,' said Claude. 'You're not. You're not like them, are you, girl?' He looked thoughtfully at her. 'You're my own dear girl, that's what you are.'

The man said loudly: 'We really must be off. We've taken up a great deal of your time already.'

'What takes up your time?' asked Claude.

The man stared at him blankly.

'What's your line of business?' persisted Claude. 'Your job? Your racket? What puts the money in your pocket?'

'I'm an insurance broker,' the man said stiffly. He grew a little red in the face. 'It's an established firm. Originally, it was my father's.'

'All our problems,' said Claude, 'our mismanaged lives, point backward to influences in childhood.'

'I dare say,' the man said. He was beginning to perspire.

'Take Lily, for instance,' continued Claude. 'When she complains that this one or that one doesn't love her, what's she really saying?'

The man fidgeted with his tie. Claude was looking straight at him, and he couldn't think how to answer. He didn't even know what the question was.

'She's saying,' said Claude, 'that *they* didn't love her. She's saying that her parents never loved her because they never could. She's saying that if they didn't love her then nobody else can, and she's saying she doesn't want anyone else to love her.'

The man stared at the floor. He felt he was in the middle of some sort of nightmare. He found the word 'love' acutely embarrassing.

'Where's the life we've lost in living, eh?' shouted Claude. 'Where are the Earls of Bushy, Bagot and Green?'

'We really must go,' the man said, speaking to his wife. 'Come on,' he ordered.

She ignored him. She was looking at the photograph. The old woman was sitting on a bench. There was a bandage round her leg . . .

insides of cheap watches, giving his last crust of bread away to those damned relations of mine. Even cousin Reub wouldn't believe the callousness that exists. Or am I being too generous on account of the blood link?

> They are slaves who fear to speak
> For the fallen or the weak,
> They are slaves who do not choose
> Hatred, suffering or abuse . . .

Oh my God, have I had my share of all three? The hatred from the women – those jealous, petty female impersonators with their tight calculating little minds and their dependence on men. During the war they hounded me from the Overseas Club – poor little me with my poor weak eyes – and still they were jealous of the way the men swarmed after me – me, with a tumour growing inside me the size of a football. How they begrudged me the solace of admiration. Teaching the men English, with my poor little education (now, which university did you attend?) and so witty and gay, giving them all leaflets for the concerts and shows, and crawling – yes, crawling – back to that concentration camp in Billing Street with Eichmann Hanna waiting for me with his bricks wrapped up in newspaper. And all of them avoiding me in the streets, all – even Reub passing me by without a look, his own blood, and not even a nod of the head, not even the courtesy of an enquiry. Once he was glad enough to acknowledge me, when he was a snotty little boy without an overcoat. 'My lovely cousin Shebah,' he would tell all his friends, and 'Can we come to the Playhouse club and watch you act? May we, please, dear Shebah?'

What money does to people! What effect it has on their ideals, their loyalties! It couldn't have happened in the old days, it just would not have happened. But now . . . now they're all alike.

This lovely house full of marvellous things, rare as peacocks, and Claude throwing his money about on drink and saying he's penniless, and Norman lying there in a suit that must have cost a fortune, though he said he couldn't afford to travel here in the train. And Lily supported from first to last by men, however she may deny it, sprawling on the grass with the sole of her shoe worn through, and her skirt held together with a safety pin. We would have been too proud to let the world see our poverty. We would have made something out of nothing and put a bit of lace here and a bit of ribbon there, and still people would have turned their heads to look at us. The hats I made out of bits of curtains and scraps of velvet, and the dresses I made out of oddments, one for every day of the week, and there wasn't an eye that didn't hold regard or envy, as I trotted down the street on my dainty little heels. When I tell them, they all say, in that annoyingly insincere way, 'Oh yes, I can believe it,' and Victorian Norman turns his head away and I'm supposed not to notice that he's laughing.

But it's true. I was unique. I was beautiful. It's the suffering, the hatred and the abuse that have brought me this low, the aloneness, the rottenness of my relations, the jealousy I've encountered everywhere. If I had received one-tenth of their education, their opportunities, what could I not have done with my life, with the brain I have. Lily's clever. She has a certain quality that I had, that makes people envious, but she uses her mind more cunningly. She wheedles and insinuates, she knows how to make herself indispensable and desirable. I never had her strength though, her sheer animal courage, which does exist, however I may disapprove. To take the risks she does, to go here, there and everywhere and have the house full of people, and to manage to appear so soft and gentle and in need of protection. I've told her all this – we even laugh about it. *Her* in need of protection! There's not a soul that comes within yards of Lily who doesn't need protecting from *her*. That poor man from the College, and that young man from America! Now *he* needed protecting, even if he was Jewish. She likes Jewish men. She likes all men. There she was inviting him to Sunday lunch served on a medley of cracked plates, and 'How do I cook this, Shebah?' and 'How should I make gravy, Shebah?' and all coy when he arrives, as if butter wouldn't melt in her mouth. Before that it had been science and atoms and explosions and, just like taking off a pair of gloves, it's medicine and psychology, and books all over the place on schizophrenia, till we were all demented. Now it's geology and rocks because of poor Edward. He's completely blinded by her, besotted, quite unable to see her true nature. Not that he isn't taking full advantage of the situation. Last night at the table he says it's his birthday, and without a sign of embarrassment he remarks he wants to spend it in bed, and up he gets and off they go – like a pair of animals.

We went for walks along the front at New Brighton, in the wind, in the rain (so beneficial to the complexion) talking, talking about literature, about art, and me in my tight little dress and a piece of fur about my neck, always talking, always walking.

We didn't go to bed all over the place, we hadn't the knowledge – we were so gay, so full of life. What they would talk about now if they hadn't the bed to retire to, God alone knows. Their pathetic bird-droppings of knowledge on books and politics and fashion. Norman with his socialistic outlook, and so concerned about the correct width of his trousers at the calf, and his uncharitable attitude towards me. Oh, I've seen him in the kitchen at

Morpeth Street, with his face flushed red, watching the girls, and he and Lily looking at one another (God knows what goes on there) and then all of a sudden it's 'Good night, all' and he winds up his clock and goes up to bed without a glance. Sometimes he did walk me home I suppose, though only because Lily told him to, and lately I can hardly bring myself to speak to him. The tickets I scrounged for him for the Film Institute, and the way he said he couldn't afford them – and that anyway he was too busy.

His mother, poor thing, doesn't understand him at all. Why should her Norman, with a good home, choose to live in one room in Morpeth Street? 'His father and I have never interfered with him,' she told me. 'He always had strange ideas.' I could have told her easily enough what sort of ideas he has, though it wouldn't have done any good. I don't want to offend him. I have to go somewhere to pass the time.

When I first met Lily I thought she was such a submissive little thing. When it gradually became apparent to me what sort of a life she was leading, and I even went so far as to call her a certain name, she merely disagreed with my choice of words. 'Tarts get paid for it,' she said. She didn't seem put out. For a moment she looked at me and her eyes held a shadow of such suffering that if it had been real, which I doubt, I might have been forced to change my opinion of her. She can look very ugly and she did then; her face was a triangle of bones. Later she cheered up and we sang songs, though she always gets the words wrong – not like me with my tremendous memory – and she begged me to sing 'The Army of Today's All Right'.

If I hadn't started to sing last night I might never have touched that glass case and Claude mightn't have shot me through the ankle. There's a moment – as I've told them so many times – when everything's too late. Of course they constantly steal my words and refuse to give me credit for them – like the night Lily, pointing at a photograph of herself and some young man in the catering trade, had the nerve to say, 'There was a moment, Shebah, when it became too late. It was to have been all happy endings, and Agonistes crowned with flowers' (whatever that might mean – her quotations are always so wildly inaccurate) 'but now I weep alone.' Weep she may have done, but hardly alone. For all that she never took down the photograph from the wall, but left it in its frame alongside the large painting of two young girls wearing white dresses with bows in their hair. Nellie and Doris, Lily called them. She'd found the painting in the basement and she put it in a gilt frame and set a vase of flowers beneath it. All that in a kitchen with the floor riddled with dry rot, or wet rot, and a samovar on the draining board, though God knows the only tea she ever made was in a pan and that stewed over and over till in the end I simply couldn't taste a normal cup of tea. It's all so changed since Lily went, though Norman has been surprisingly kind. I used to sit in the basket chair under the picture of the cabin boy with his faded midshipman's cap, and opposite the painting of Nellie and Doris. Of course I do still sit in the same chair when I visit Norman, but Lily took all the pictures away with her. If she wanted to create an impression, though God knows she could hardly fail to do that, Lily would tell her visitors that she liked to think of Nellie and Doris safely through their dual menopause and dead and buried. 'It gives, don't you think' (a wide, candid smile) 'such perspective to our lives?' And they, the fools, just gaped at her and of course came again and again. Had they known, had they dreamt of the way she would dissect them once they'd left, they wouldn't have thought her quite so innocent, so much the child. There was another photograph, quite small, of her dead father, hung between a Russian farming family and the entry of the Germans into Vienna. Her poor father was such a polite man, and intelligent enough to recognise me as a lady, and there again the general attitude was so bewildering, so eccentric.

I thought of Lily that entire fog-wreathed day of her father's funeral, as I struggled through the streets hardly able to breathe, nearly knocked down by a No. 12 bus, mourning with her, saying a little prayer for the departed. And then to arrive later that night at Morpeth Street only to find the kitchen crowded and Lily with a fur hat on and a blanket and a pair of Wellington boots, behaving as if she was drunk, which she may have been. Not one expression of sorrow, not one tear, not one glance of respect or sympathy, merely an air of hilarity, of thanksgiving. Miss Evans – the hair-removing woman – and myself were the only ones who shed a tear for fathers lost and fathers gone (though hers by the sound of him was no loss to the bogs of Ireland), and I remembered, if indeed I had ever forgotten, how ill I was when *my* dear father died. They were all laughing, and Lizzie had been attacked coming through the streets, and Norman had given her a sip of brandy (the money they throw about), and Lily told a dreadful story about how her father sometimes hadn't spoken for months and how the Vicar had said he was a jolly man. She sat there in that fur hat of hers, with lines of dirt about her mouth, drinking stewed tea and loving it all. Because of the fog no one could go home and they all paired off like animals as usual, and I was told to go and lie down on the sofa (Miss Evans for some reason having pressed to take the brass bed), and when I left Lily was lying on a lilo on the kitchen floor in her hat and boots singing, 'Oh, it's nice to have a home of your own.' I don't mean to be critical – she can be a kind child – but sometimes her callousness is appalling. I won't say she's been callous to me, not really, though I daresay she can be behind my back, and having heard her views on all her friends, so-called, I don't see why I should be exempt, but she does tend to adopt a different attitude in front of different people. Claude for instance seemed to bring out the worst in her. He used to arrive without warning at Morpeth Street – just get into his yellow motor car and drive all those miles and arrive with bottles of this and bottles of that – and for days Lily would be laughing and shouting, altogether too elated. Of course elation is only the extreme end of deep depression, but how she kept going all through the day, what with her job to go to and the telephone ringing, and rifling the gas meters for money to buy eggs and tea, and the nights spent in abandonment, I shall never understand. I came one afternoon, because I was passing the door and wanted to make sure of my appointment with Lily for the evening, and there was Claude in the kitchen, stretched out on my chair with a glass in front of him. He said, 'Hallo, my dear, you look well' – me, hardly able to lift my head for the pain and the tragedy of everything, the ignorant swine – and there was this old, old creature with bedroom slippers on its feet, and hands caked with dirt, rocking back and forth like a rag doll. Lily said, 'Shebah, this is Miss Charters. She's a friend of mine,' as if in some way we had something in common. Oh, I felt pity for the poor old thing, so neglected and so idiotic, asking me if my daddy went to sea, but they simply don't see the difference between my suffering with the brain I've got, and these other vermin who barely inhabit the earth. I wish to God I could wallow in my muck and accept all that England has to offer. I did try, but I couldn't bring myself to talk to her at all, and afterwards Lily said I had been impolite to Miss Charters, and Claude gave a little high-pitched laugh and began to whistle between his teeth. I can't afford to be too rude to Lily, but sometimes I would like to tell her dear devoted friends exactly what she thinks of them behind their backs. I know it was kind of Claude to invite me here, even if it was only for target practice, but I've done my share of entertaining. I've ceaselessly provided them with knowledge. And there was the train fare and peppermints for Julia, and I did sit and pat those damn dogs for half an hour.

It could have been so charming, this weekend, in this ideal setting, the place so beautifully furnished and the pictures everywhere, but almost from the moment we arrived there were undertones and atmospheres and one or other of them would vanish into another room and whisper away, or there would be looks at each other, and those tedious half-finished sentences, like the half of a letter you find in the street, that you can't make head nor tail of, no matter how you try. It's as if all this fascination with sex builds a big wall betwixt the devotees and the non-devotees. If you aren't a participant there's simply so much that's incomprehensible. They pretend to be interested in art and politics and books, and they seem to chat quite intelligently for a time, but always, like a maggot eating its way across a particularly decayed and juicy fruit, there's this sexual business, leaving a small trail of slime, and nothing else seems really to bring them to life. I do see, now that Lily has explained it to me, that it's not entirely what it seems. Even I can see that their motives are somewhat different, but their impulses all seem to be working in unison, and they all pretend so much to emotions that must surely be real only once, that must be true only the first time, not over and over like a ball unable to stop bouncing.

When we came through the door of the shop yesterday, Claude put his arms round Lily and they clung there among all those breakable things set out on mahogany tables, mouths emitting sucking noises and Julia behind them, so courteous, so well bred. To look at her you would never dream she was a *mistress*, that she too was indulging so vividly and with such ladylike capability in this orgy of shared eroticism, night after night taking off her spectacles and brushing her hair, and rub-rub-rubbing at those lovely teeth, and after that God knows what madness. The way they all attend to their teeth, as if *they* were the gates to some sort of parkland. Reub has good teeth, though he speaks with his lips close together, spitting out his facts and figures and percentages, and once when he had the generosity to take me over the road for a cup of coffee, he yawned, and I had a glimpse of the lining of his mouth and his back molars were glittering with gold. I ought to have my teeth attended to, I really ought – but oh, the shame of exposing the private, altogether too intimate cavities of the jaw to some jumped-up little dentist boy, and I can't quite see myself going round with a mouth full of dentures, artificial snapping like a mad dog, and they would have to be kept decent and cleaned day and night and it's all too much trouble for poor me. It's all too loose in there. It's like a purse with the lining in threads. I've seen Lily spewing blood out after she's cleaned her teeth at night, and mixing stuff in a glass and swilling it round her mouth and tears starting from her eyes.

She does look ill. It's all this racketing about and not eating properly and rushing from place to place. It's extraordinary how particular they are about their emotions and their teeth, and yet they simply never eat a decent meal or sleep regularly. Julia did provide a very nice meal for us last night, though it was ruined by conversation. When I think of how my poor mother prepared a meal – such care, such bravery in the face of adversity. Not that she would stoop to cook anything so simple as shepherd's pie.

And the wine Claude kept offering, running like water, and the indiscreet sentences tossed between them . . .

'It's a bloody wonderful life,' said Norman. He's right there – it is for *him*, with his weekly wage and his doting mother.

'You mean that?' Claude, the fool, stares entranced as if discovering great wisdom.

'Yes. Yes, I do. I live, I make love to as many women as possible, I eat well, I climb mountains. I've good friends and we had a damn good time all together in Morpeth Street.'

'I reckon,' said Claude, for some reason agreeing with Norman, 'that you're right. I reckon love-making is about all a man should want. That and drink, eh?'

With a boozy surge of laughter they raised their glasses to be refilled, and listened to his oratory.

'I reckon that in order for the blood to flow, we must have real stimulation. It's all right for some people, with their diamond minds . . .'

'Oh darling,' I cried, for who else could Claude have meant but me, staring at me like that with his sweet, crazy eyes, 'but the rest of us ordinary mortals need something in which to sublimate ourselves – some way in which we can release our inhibitions and return to the soil.'

The words evidently had an effect on Lily's young man. He stood up calmly and commanded Lily to go to bed with him. There and then, without more ado. Wanted to celebrate his birthday, he said, in the most fitting way. And Lily sitting there with a little satisfied smile as if he were paying her a compliment instead of insulting her. And we were left sitting round the table in the kitchen, talking trivialities and they drinking their wine, and me feeling so weary and far too polite to mention it.

'Come, come Shebah,' Claude said, 'the night is young.' And

I couldn't disagree with him, being a guest in his house – and anyway I didn't want to imply that I wasn't young.

For I am young, far younger than them. I used to sit up all night during the war, in the shelters, and when even that poor refuge was denied me by the attitude of the scum who came there, I would huddle in a blanket on my little divan in my room high above the street, a sort of Jewish barrage balloon, my stomach all swollen with the tumour inside me. I did have my own little room – though I only moved there just for somewhere to put my things, never intending to stop twenty years – with all my books on the shelves, some with inscriptions written just inside the cover in *his* handwriting. 'Did you ever have a love affair?' asked Claude last night. Did I ever have a love affair! You'd think they had a monopoly on love. Maybe not what they would call an affair, though that did happen once, but it was a romantic affair, and it was more than enough for me. How they stand the repeated strain on the nerves, and the intrigue and the heartache I can't imagine, let alone the echo they must evoke deep within their minds of similar words uttered in similar situations and for similar ends. My affair was so rich in texture, so varied in its detail.

There I sat at a play-reading and the hall was mostly in darkness because that was the way the director of the dramatic society wanted it done, and I was reciting some lines and *he* heard my voice, and *he* said to a friend, there and then in the pitch blackness, 'My God, who's she? I must know her.' *He* had seen me about of course, everybody had, and I was so different and so chic, but we hadn't actually spoken. After that night *he* bought me flowers and we sat for hours talking about poetry. *He* had such a sombre face, a dark face with studious eyes, and so tall and educated. When I think of those things Lily called men who used to court her, that little toad of an American – Joel or Moley or something – and that professor all fourteen stone of fat, or that Billie with his schoolboy face and blubbery eyes – in comparison with *him*, I smile. She doesn't know what a man is. And I wouldn't let him buy me as much as a cup of tea, because I was too proud. The night he introduced me to his wife I was so charming, and she said to him later, 'I love Shebah. You should love Shebah too. She is so different, so alive.' Of course all the other hags in the readers' circle were jealous of me and wouldn't speak to me. There was a positive gathering up of the folds of the skirts if I came too near, and all the men flocked round me and thought me something I most definitely was not. I wonder what stopped me. I could have been like Lily. God knows I flirted enough. I was so gay, so painfully exhilarated, with those great eyes of mine giving me such hell even then. I was too vain to wear glasses, though I was almost blind. The pain I endured. *He* thought I was weeping, and observed I was too tender for this world, which in a way I was, though it was mostly my eyes were so damn weak.

I shall never forget the day I came into the club, long after we had severed our association, and the men were sitting by the fire talking and Mr Cohen said, because he knew – they all knew – 'Isn't it terrible, Shebah?' and I said, 'What?' and Mr Cohen said, 'Why, *he's* gassed himself, Shebah.'

And then I did weep, and I don't care what they thought. I never liked Jewish men. Never. Always the Christian boys. Besides, my poor father would never have been able to give me a dowry, and I hated the idea of being bought. And the Christian men were too stupid except *him*, though there was probably a touch of the Jew there, with those eyes, and I could never understand women wanting to have children. The responsibility it must entail. The strength it must require. And then there's always the worry: that time Lily nearly died – though she never told me the full story. How she coped with the worry I'll never know. And no sooner is she through with that than she meets the American with his stony face and I warned her, because I do have a deep regard for her even if I think her a damn fool. 'Don't give yourself to him, darling,' I warned.

She laughed, with those innocent eyes shining like baubles and said, 'Why, Shebah, I love him, I love him.' At least that's what she called it. There she is asking me round to Sunday dinner and asking me if I've brought the black bread and setting out the food on three cracked plates and music on the gramophone and not a mention of Billie and all that love.

Oh no, it's schizophrenia and the mid-brain and diseases of the kidney from morning till night, and arguments about the medical service both here and on the continent, and such coyness. Though what that American made of it all I don't know. Thought he was in a typically British household, God help him, and quite bewildered and glassy-eyed – what with Victorian Norman spouting Communism at him, and that dreadful man Rafferty arriving drunk and begging to see Our Kid and telling everyone he's a navy man, and Claude coming in his frock coat to commit suicide and the Professor breaking his atomic heart on the front step. The American had the cheek to tell me I was completely *sane*. Poor little me with my tragic life and all the torment of visiting the out-patients' department every week. 'Have you ever had a day by the sea?' he asked me. A day by the sea! The poor fool. Of course Lily made out he was a doctor, but what the hell did he know? Anyway, the atomic professor's darling books on neutrons were parcelled up, and then we had volumes all over the place on Elation and new approaches to Manic

Depressives (God knows, I've been one of those for years without having books on it) and case books on Psycho-analysis until no one hardly ever spoke, just came in and sat down and started reading and imagining all sorts of things. Everyone had had such terrible childhoods and no one had experiences any more, only traumas. Not that the American made us very welcome all the time he was around. Just standing, all four feet of him by the sink, with folded arms, the breathing example of an inferiority complex, saying 'Yeah' and 'Nope' to whatever one said, and no sense of humour at all. Then when he had gone and the light had gone out of Lily's eyes, she seemed worried again, though of course she's so deep and it might just have been tiredness.

There's something wrong now, but I don't suppose I'll be permitted to know. If only she knew how trustworthy I am! I did think last night that Claude was going to confide in me, but he didn't tell me very much. 'Come, Shebah,' he says, and I prepared myself for one of his ridiculous conversations which aren't conversations at all but recitations about his wife leaving him (God knows, one can hardly blame her) and the great glory that is Lily, and a few flatteries thrown at me, just as if I can't see through him, or any of them. And there was Victorian Norman with his arm round Julia while she washed the dishes.

'Shall I help you, darling?' I said, bloody fool that I am, hardly able to stand, and offering to clean their china for them.

'No, thank you, Shebah,' Julia says, mouth impeccably shaping her vowels, steam from the bowl blurring her glasses so that I couldn't see her expression, though I can imagine it. She wanted me out of the way so as to be alone with Norman.

When I used to help at the Overseas Club during the war the rotten women were so jealous of me. All the young men wanted to talk with me, to be with Shebah. 'Teach us to speak English,

Shebah,' they would say. 'You speak English so beautifully.' And those women with their wretched little brains said, 'No thank you, Shebah, there's nothing for you to do, we can manage.' They're all alike, God forgive them.

So Claude and I go upstairs, under that angel made of wood, into the long living-room, and he puts on the gramophone (how they all dote on noise) and I settle myself on the sofa. There was a little time taken up with those moist dogs and I had to pat them and he kept saying 'Lie down' all the time, inciting them to jump around with saliva dripping from their great purple jaws, and I went on laughing and making soothing noises, though really I wanted to scream. After a time he got tired of all that, and they put their noses into the carpet and went off to sleep. 'Dear Shebah,' he said, 'how you observe us all . . . how wise you are.' He really is a most interesting man, even if he did shoot me down in the grass. A puckish face, rather creased, and merry eyes and that beard in little curls so that he constantly licks out at tendrils with his tongue, and a small mouth, very pink. How young they all look in spite of their complications. So deeply healthy.

'What, me?' I said, because I detest insincere flattery, and he wagged his head, which is a whimsical habit of his, and repeated, 'How wise you are', and stares down at my feet. At the end of my legs (oh, my shapely legs that danced so much, that walked so far) I could see my sandals swing above the carpet and my little toes peeping out, and a dab of sealing-wax that was really red nail-varnish blobbing one toe and just visible through my stocking. My pathetic adornments. Reub said it was the harlot in me, the swine.

'What about you,' I trilled, 'with all this beauty round you, and your wonderful knowledge – aren't you wise?'

Which certainly wasn't wise of me because it meant Claude could start on about his wife leaving him, etc., etc., but I had to say something. After a while he said, 'You see, the wise ones are those who no longer fight against life, but accept and observe.' And he licked at his beard again and pushed at one of the dogs with his foot, though mercifully it remained unconscious. They all say some very clever things and very important things, but their method of delivery is so bad. I keep trying to tell Lily this, but it's something they can't understand. Being an actress I say things with conviction. You do have to dramatise when making the profounder statements. Anyway, Claude looks so well fed and so cushioned with grandeur that it's simply absurd to think of him fighting against anything. What on earth is there for him to object to? If only he had paused or sighed in the appropriate place I would have been more convinced. I know he's had his troubles, his sufferings, though God knows he's done it in comfort, in opulence, but the art of conversation is communication, and communication is a thing that must be felt. The spoken word seems to have lost its meaning. With all this television any little chit of a nothing walking the streets can mouth about life and suffering. Take that girl in the Kardomah some months ago, with her hair bleached and frizzed about her ears – quite attractive really, with her smooth little face devoid of expression. I had gone in for a cup of tea (I have to sit somewhere and the G.P.O. was about to close and I was too early for my next appointment and so weary) and there was this common man sitting by the wall, slouched in his chair, with a face stamped with brutality and weakness, such as they all bear marks of now, being kept and housed and fed by England and no need to work at all. I hadn't been there for more than a few moments and had brought the edge of my cup to my mouth, about to drink, when I saw this lout put two spoons and a knife into the pocket of his jacket. He saw me looking at him and we stared at one another, a quite exquisite second of perception, me with my cup held up and he with his hand curled round the cutlery in his pocket, and all the little cafe sounds about us – hot water rushing out of the urn, the saucers being rattled – and a moment of recognition between this sot and myself. Then he got up, still with his eyes fixed on mine, and in a moment I was standing by the exit with my poor weak arms outstretched, weary as I was. Nobody moved, though people looked up from their crumbling buns. 'No, you don't,' I shouted. 'Thief, taker of property.' The fools on the counter just stared at me, lifeless, immobile. 'He's put Kardomah cutlery into his pocket, two spoons and a knife – I saw him. Call the manager,' I shouted. I knew there wasn't much point in calling the manager, because he was most likely upstairs threshing about among the cardboard boxes and sacks of sugar, commingling with one of the women assistants. The man, the thief, just moved forward and took hold of my arm and thrust me roughly aside, and in a moment he was in the revolving doors and round and out with a damp rush of air into the darkling street. Just went, and nobody came to my assistance. Down went the insensitive heads to the currant scones and the mugs of tea, and this little fool with the dyed and curled hair, as transparent as a piece of glass, said softly in a voice distorted with catarrh, 'Ah, give him a chance. Aren't you human?'

Just that. 'Aren't you human?' Had it been reversed, had it been I who had stolen so much as a crust of bread, they would have trampled on me, risen in a pyramid of loathing from the tables and ground me to the floor, called me a dirty Jew, cast me into prison. It was on account of the feeling and the emotion that I put into my accusation that they hated me. They sat with an embarrassment that turned them to stone. It is the generation of the unemphatic. Steal, kill, lie, fornicate, but beware of indulging with conviction. That's their idea of being human.

Anyway, Claude's quite wrong. I've never stopped fighting. I've never accepted so much as a cup of water. I've fought all my life for justice and been broken and destroyed in its cause. However, I suppose Claude was meaning to pay me a compliment when he said I was wise, etc., etc., and I couldn't tell him to go to bloody hell as I would have liked, seeing I was a guest in his house of china, so I contented myself with 'Oh darling. Me – accepting? How little you know.' Which of course only made him feel how humble I was, though as usual with all of them I got the impression that he was only half concentrating, that he was waiting or listening for something else. If I wasn't so subtle I would have decided long ago that they were all deliberately trying to humiliate and torment me, which is true in a way, but really it's their thoughtlessness and their preoccupation with sex.

To which he replied, fiddling and tugging at his curled beard, 'Very perceptive, my dear, very perceptive. How little I know! But this I do know. While we have sat on this sofa this five minutes, twelve people somewhere have died of hunger. Died starving.'

I want to scream when they start talking this way. It's so debasing. Are they talking to me or to themselves? Do I look as if I'm one of the privileged, that they have to relate the statistics of little yellow people clutching rice bowls? It's not my concern. I have enough to battle with in my own monstrous head without problems of that sort. Not that they do anything about the hungry either. It's all talk. And if I haven't starved to death it's no thanks to anybody but myself. I haven't been lend-leased or subsidised, and I don't have the solace of their endless involvements. I've had nothing but loneliness and jealousy and ill health. I feel as if I'm constantly struggling under a net cast carelessly by a careless God. I'm the only one I know enmeshed in it, all the others move freely. The appalling thing is that nobody seems aware of my plight.

Once when that landlord of mine, the Panzer man in the tennis pumps, had thrown bricks at me, I ran out screaming into the road. 'Help, murder,' I shouted. People passed by on foot with shut faces, and people went past in the glass cabins of their cars, eyes unseeing, and no one lifted a finger of surprise. The landlord came down the steps with his bicycle under his arm and propped it against the railings while he fixed his cycle clips round the frayed bottoms of his trousers. He mounted his machine, and the white tennis shoes, black laces dangling, trod round and round on the pedals and carried him out of sight. He, of course, had his own sedatives, his rotten Irish Catholic candle-lighting, and his paid women who came nightly, spiking up the uncarpeted stairs in their high-heeled shoes, their very breathing sulphurous with corruption. But I have nothing, no compensations, no curtain of deceit to hide myself from myself – only my poor brain endlessly facing itself. Claude's remark was only to be expected, because they always make such comments, so I shouldn't have felt so irritated, so exhausted with bitterness. Knowing so much, my bitterness can only be self-directed, there being nobody worthier to receive it. I had to sit there nodding agreement, rolling my eyes while the blood pounded in my head. There was a small silence in which the record ended. Lily used to have a gramophone in the kitchen, and two records which she played every evening. The battery on my nerves was simply frightful. It's not that I can't enjoy music – who better? – but my appointments were for communication, as I used to tell her, not to have to shout my thoughts above a cyclone of violins. I didn't want Claude to put on another orchestral work, so I said as quickly as I could before he noticed the silence, 'Do you think, Claude darling, that Edward is right for her?'

Then he said a most extraordinary thing. I suppose it was only extraordinary in that there's so much I'm never told. It's like trying to complete a jigsaw. They toss me all the edges but never the most vital pieces in the centre.

'It's not a question of rightness, Shebah. He's needed very much. And I reckon in some ways he'll do.'

'What do you mean – needed?' I hate begging them for explanations, but I was so taken by surprise.

'Well . . . ' He pursed up his little wet mouth and let his chin rest on his chest so that his face was mostly beard and there were plumes of auburn hair springing out of his scalp. Then up comes his head and he puts a large hand on my black-skirted knee and stares at me intently. Really quite dramatic, considering what they're usually like. 'Don't we all need someone, or something?' he says, the fool, the sly antique dealer, talking to me as if I worked in a factory or was one of those ignorant little things he picks up in his yellow van. They do belittle my intelligence so. He meant of course something different, but until Lily actually confides in me, or until the faint rumours begin to circulate, I'll never know. Which left me in pain again. Suffocating pain, because I have no outlet for my passion, and the less I can project my passion into words, the more I sense the threat of nothingness. And then he began to talk about the glory that is Lily, which was interesting in one way and not entirely drivel. He said, 'Of us all, Lily needs nobody. I say this guardedly. The rest of us can find our little treadwheel and go round and round, because basically all we care about is stupefying ourselves.

Intensity of life can be found equally well in business or in drink.'

Here I said sharply, because I wasn't going to let him get away with it, 'And the so-called loving you all indulge in?'

Here his eyes flickered – once, twice – beneath lids tinted pink. He removed his hand from my knee and commenced to tug at his beard worriedly. 'No, no, Shebah, that's something quite different. We none of us indulge, as you call it, for the reasons you believe. Some for loneliness, some for forgetfulness, some because they are endlessly chosen.' The skin of his face wasn't after all so very young, so extremely healthy. 'But, you see, Lily has chosen life. She's the self-creator of her own struggling, her own griefs, her own happiness. She endures self-loss only to fling herself triumphantly back into an emotional battle to regain herself. She won't, she can't – seeing she's the only contestant – give in. That's the glory of her.'

Well, I couldn't laugh out loud in his face, and I hadn't the energy to start a futile discussion, so again I nodded my poor aching head, and he seemed satisfied and with a little sigh, whether real or assumed, stood up and went downstairs trailing his hand on the surface of the wall.

The rubbish they talk. Lily has chosen life. She's the self-creator. It's almost as if he thought Lily religious. Of course she's a Catholic, or was, though that was probably a decision taken on impulse. All that business of riding on a tram up or down a hill to a convent in the mist, and joining the nuns at prayer, and letting salt tears run down her cheeks. How her senses must have grovelled before the little lighted candles and the rising voices, really not unlike Blackpool during the illuminations, and the incense burning, and imagining herself in ecstasy and full of divine grace. Her whole existence is a catalogue of sensual indulgences. She's never self-created anything, only gone blindly into any situation that presented itself. I was there that night the Billie man called on some pretext. I was sitting in the kitchen by appointment and long before his knock came she confided that somebody might arrive – no one of any importance she stressed, purely a matter of business – but would I mind going upstairs and resting on the bed in the bathroom for a little time, should a visitor come. And before she would open the door to him I was bundled upstairs with all my parcels and my carrier bag, still holding a plate of stew in my hand and hardly able to see in the badly-lit hall. I could hear voices, and then there was some banging and then there was silence. I stayed up there as long as I could, as long as was humanly possible, what with the cold and all the insane people rushing in to use the lavatory and their crazy comments, and when I did go back into the kitchen, the panel under the sink was open and there was water all over the floor and on the floor amid the potato peelings and the swillage, grovelled Lily and her Billie – what an absurd concatenation. Such a different Lily from the one half an hour before, eyes shining, mouth curved in a tender smile, really very pretty, with her skirt marked and stained with tea leaves, and he the great fool, red in the face and a piece of sticking plaster stuck on his dimpled chin. I never liked Billie. When he had gone she sat with her face in her hands, in the midst of all that mess, rocking backwards and forwards. 'I love him,' she said, though she wasn't telling me, 'I love him, I love him.' Since that time she's jumped on the same chair quite a few times and repeated the same sentiments, only about different people. The fact that she emerges triumphantly, as Claude describes it, out of all these situations, isn't courage but luck. Supreme good fortune. And the opportunities she has had! I sat there last night quite alone, and only a few yards away lay Lily with her latest lover, adrift in each other's arms. God knows what passes through her mind at such moments. There was never anywhere I could go. I couldn't get up from the table and announce I was spending a birthday in bed; I possessed no friends who openly encouraged me.

I went all the way to London so many years ago, by coach, with Monica Sidlow (she hated me too, with her over-active glands, which deposited fat all over her hips and thighs) and we stayed at some theatrical boarding house for one night, before she went on to Paris. What a sight she looked, pouring water into a basin, great arms a-flurry with flesh, and the short muscular legs bare and pallid under the laced camisole. I could have gone to Paris with her, only even then there didn't seem any difference – Paris, London, all one – I had to take myself with me wherever I went. My love, my married man with the grey calm eyes and the wife who had after all told him to adore me, was coming down by car to fetch me. When *he* did come I stood as if facing an army, a whole regiment of enemies with loaded guns pointing at my breast, with a fearful excitement building up inside me, and I shouted, 'Don't dare touch me,' so violently that people in the street turned to look at us.

And he, one long grenadier, his noble face white in the hurrying street, said – pleaded – entreated, 'What do you want, Shebah? For God's sake, what do you want?'

He had a coat (he always dressed most beautifully) made of some dark textured cloth, and the fingers of his right hand touched the lapels nervously, while he stood looking at me. I said, still shouting, 'Nothing, nothing from you,' and he turned away and walked very slowly back to his big green car, and I didn't wait to see him drive away, but buttoned up my little black gloves and pushed the fur of my collar higher around my ears and trotted as fast as my legs would carry me into the unknown crowds. For a time my exultation was so magnificent that I could have walked all day, but gradually the feeling left me and my mouth became dry, and I was after all alone, having accomplished a gesture of nothingness. Why, I ask myself, did I behave like that? Of course I did want something from him; I suppose I was in love with him. Of course he wasn't mine, he did belong to his wife, and in those days that counted for much, but it wasn't entirely that. Perhaps it's because I'm bigger than anyone I've ever met. There's so much of me that there's no room for transference. Perhaps it's the Jewish wandering element in me. A wanderer over the face of the earth. As a baby, a tiny Hebrew-nosed infant, with weak eyes closed shut, my mother carried me across Russia. And what hell she went through with my father's relations! Always walking, always on the move. Even now I can't keep still, I have to keep going, even if it's only round and round the blackened streets of the town. I could never tell Lily (because though she might be moved by its symbolic beauty at the time of telling, later she would repeat it to all and sundry, and distort its meaning beyond recall), but it is *his* coat I remember now more than his face. His lovely dark majestic coat. I'm truly the self-creator of my own struggles. Impulsive it may appear, but underneath there's an inflexible will that guides my destiny. That's my great glory – damn, damn them.

I wondered last night what was up between Norman and Julia. She seems very sweet – but you never know, and Norman is capable of anything. Lily has told me that Norman is the only man she has ever met who wanted sex for the real reason, what she calls the biological urge. Or maybe I've got it wrong. Maybe it was Norman she was talking about when she said he'd use a keyhole if it was handy. If she told Claude that, it's a wonder he left Julia alone with Norman, though perhaps Claude wouldn't mind. They're all so deep. Why now, should he shoot me this morning? I don't get the impression, though I could be wrong, that Claude has an inflexible will that rules his existence. And if he has, it wouldn't seem enough reason to aim a gun at poor me with my countless torments, and pull the trigger. I haven't done him so much harm, and if I have it was his fault forcing me to drink, though if I hadn't drunk I would have wept.

After our little discussion last night Claude was downstairs quite a while. It was almost pleasant sitting there among all those marvellous bits and pieces. I was slightly anxious in case the dogs woke up and started their antics, but I sat very still with my hands folded, and when Claude came back up the stairs with Norman and Julia (both very elated and gay) he shouted out, 'Ho, my dear, you look like an African carving . . . better have a drink.' Norman was laughing a great deal and wriggling about in his clothes and blowing his nose over and over into a spotless handkerchief. The noise he made.

'We're going to sing "Happy Birthday" to the loved ones,' shouted Claude, filling up glasses on the piano top.

So we all trooped to the door and down two little steps and stood outside another door, very old, with a great iron hinge (everything's too perfect) and Claude started up the chorus. We made a great volume of sound, but I'm not so unobservant as not to notice how close Victorian Norman was standing to Julia, and how his fingers kept digging into her neck, and all the time shouting at the top of his voice, 'Happy Birthday, dear Edward.' It was very stimulating. Even I felt slightly absorbed, because it was an absorbing thing to do, disturbing them like that.

Behind the door I could hear Lily laughing. Of course she had to laugh just to show there was no ill-feeling, and Claude put his hand on the latch of the door and would have gone in, only Julia said protestingly, 'No, Claude, no,' and we all went back into the other room still singing. It was so simple to have another drink; I felt through drink that I might be more included, not so dreadfully impaled upon my own character and personality.

'Why don't you sing Lily's song?' said Norman, damn him, hunching his narrow shoulders and walking rapidly up and down the room. So I did. Heaven knows I've sung it often enough in the past. I sang it because I like to have a rousing chorus, though I think to Lily it represented a kind of comfort to the heart. Years ago Lily invited me round for the evening of the Day of Atonement. It wasn't my usual appointment night, but she said come round anyway, because she can be kind, and all my people had deserted me, and it was a time of great sadness for me. When I went into the kitchen there were candles, and hanging from the ceiling a gaudy red star made out of shiny paper, a Christmas decoration, and I felt like saying 'I'm a Jew, not a Communist', and on the table plates with little rolls of bread on them with scraps of sardines inside, and a gherkin on a saucer. On the draining board there was a bottle of whisky and a bottle of wine. So typical to have spent so much on drink and so little on food!

'Oh darling,' I said, 'why the celebration?' All my people were fasting and praying that night, but she just smiled and said, 'Happy birthday, Shebah' (what fools they all are), and I put my bundles down on the green velvet chair, absolutely mesmerised by that great shining scarlet star, hanging on a thread of cotton from a hook in the stained ceiling. 'I have a surprise for you,' she told me, leading me up the hall and into the living-room. There on the purple sofa, reading a book, was Claude with a thin emaciated face, appearing almost holy. Of course I knew he'd been sick, but I'd thought he was in some sort of mental home, and he said, quite unlike himself, 'Hallo, Shebah', and gravely regarded me out of saintly eyes. He looked as if he were some figure on a tomb, with his two little feet neatly together and his beard in a little point, and a gown in neat folds about his body. It was all so unexpected. People kept arriving and bringing things, chocolate raisins and bottles of wine and a bag of nuts, and them all wishing me happy birthday in that insane way and getting very drunk.

We had to stay in the kitchen on account of Claude needing peace and quiet, but one or other of us would trip along every now and then to the cool of his lying-in room, and we all thought how changed he was, how like St Sebastian, St Joseph or Christ, all except Lily who refused to comment, just went on drinking wine and talking to her American by the sink. He stood with his arms folded, hardly uttering a word. Poor devil, arrested against the draining board, subjugated to Lily and ten thousand dreams of American superiority tinkling invisible to ruin among the debris in the sink. He wouldn't go and see Claude at all. Once when Lily was about to take some bread to Claude, he said in that inhuman drawl, 'I reckon he's had enough attention', and she ate the roll herself. Of course she does adopt this complacent feminine attitude with all her lovers, which may fool them but hardly fools me. Victorian Norman was on the floor, almost under the table with Lizzie's friend Patricia, whispering into her ear with the perspiration running down his face. Lizzie was sitting on her boy-friend's knee, really a very sweet girl, though just like all of them. And Lily so fond of her, which is strange because she's quite pretty, and in the end I expect she'll do Lily down. They all do. I never liked Lizzie's boy-friend, not a nice man, almost dreadful but saved by a sense of humour, always more than ready to insult me. He sang 'The Holly and the Ivy' in a trained voice, shifting his eyes from side to side throughout, a cup of whisky clasped in his hand. Then I sang 'Let's Start All Over Again', and they clapped and made loud noises of appreciation, all except the American Statue of Liberty, who gazed coldly at us out of sloe-shaped eyes, dry as prunes. Of course he was Jewish. Little Lizzie went in to see Claude and was away rather a long time and the boy-friend padded along the hall to fetch her. Voices were raised in anger. Then they both returned, he with a face suffused with annoyance, saying Claude wasn't all that sick, and she patting his crimson cheeks mouthing 'There, there', as if comforting a child. They all have so much physical contact. Hours went by in a rustle of undeciphered murmurings, a tracery of fingers endlessly stroking heads of hair, a dozen licentious violet mouths pursed up to imprint kisses on each other. Winding together, all of them, even poor saintly Claude new to his mortification, touching, clinging, reaching. How apart I sat, how alien. They all live coupled lives and I alone am singular, isolated. Of course the Professor when he was visiting Lily didn't maul her in front of me, but then he was too bewildered. He used to come sometimes for lunch and coincide with the policeman. No one ever explained why the policeman called. Surely not him as well! He used to chain his cycle to the railings outside, and Norman said we should be thankful he wasn't in the mounted division. The Professor sat locked in a prison of detachment. His vast body overlapped his upright chair. Only his eyes remained alert, dismayed, drowned in their own philandering. He accepted his mug of stewed tea with disbelief, while Lily, supreme in her slum kitchen, hummed for my benefit something from Gilbert and Sullivan. She always has a line of song for every occasion, sung badly of course, but comical. She told me that the day she was born, her moment of entry into life, the Bolton Borough Band were on the wireless and a Mr Gearn was giving a euphonium solo. All lies but very interesting. And she said miles away, under the earth in the Llay Main Colliery in Wales, a boy was working, and just as her mother shuddered in the final birth pangs, a piece of steel flew out of a wedge and opened this particular boy's jugular vein, so that he expired on the instant. I suppose it's possible. She asked me when I was born. She was bored, because for once there were no men calling and though she pretends to be cultural she has no consistency, and we sat hunched over that blue oilcloth on the table and she wrote things down on a scrap of paper. She's so convincing that I did begin to tremble slightly with a kind of excitement, as if there would really be some clue as to why my life has been one of such suffering and torment. I was a bit wary at first of giving the true year of my birth. It sounded so ancient, so pre-existent – October 29th, 1899. I flounced a little and evaded her question but finally she made me tell her and I regretted it immediately, because I'm sure she's told everybody. I don't know why she makes me tell her things. God knows, no one else would even dare to ask. Anyway, she wrote down the date and then counted on her fingers (there seem such gaps in her education) and looked up knowingly, 'Ah that's interesting. Three nines are most interesting . . . ' What rubbish. 'Why, darling?' I said, humouring her, but all the same there was a little bead of terror and delight rolling through my bloodstream. 'Well, it leaves 18 and 2, which makes 20.' At least she added it up correctly. 'So take 20 from the three nines, or 27, and what have we?' she asked. 'We've seven left,' I said, while her pencil went on doodling across the paper. She was drawing a great clump of flowers in and out of all the dates.

'Exactly,' she said. 'At seven years of age there was a great change in your life, and one that influenced you throughout the years that followed.' Of course I must have told her at some time how my poor father left London and came to the north just before my seventh birthday, and how I went to the Hebrew school, and how I felt I was forever doomed to unhappiness. That was the year I knew I was unique and singled out for some great destiny. Of course I never imagined just what kind of destiny. I thought it was something glorious, something miraculous. I didn't dream that greatness was a word that could be equally well applied to states of poverty and misery. However, I said, 'Go on, darling, that's clever,' though clever it was not.

'What hour were you born?' she asked, staring at me as if she believed I was mesmerised by her. I can never tell if she's acting or not. 'In the afternoon,' I said, though God knows if I was correct. Who the bloody hell cares now – certainly not my poor dear mother, gone beyond recall. There I was, an orphan, for all I had been born of parents in 1899, talking such rubbish with a chit of a girl whose egotism is only exceeded by mine.

'Well,' she went on, 'let me see.' And there was a little silence during which I may have laughed scornfully though now I can't remember. 'Right,' she said quite loudly, and sat up straight and laid her pencil down on the piece of paper. 'At the moment of near birth two cousins chose to marry not far from your home. An Albert Cohen and a Georgina Goldberg. They stood in the Empress Rooms at the Kensington Palace Hotel and were married by the Rabbi and two assistants. At the Lyceum, Henry Irving was applying powder to his brow during the matinée interval of *Robespierre*. At the Shaftesbury Theatre the stage was being swept for the evening performance of the *Belle of New York*. The Boers had been bombarding Mafeking for two hours, and would continue to do so for another two, managing to kill one dog, breed unknown. The dear Queen went out for a drive with Princess Henry of Battenberg, and remarked that the weather was mild. General Harrison, ex-president of the U.S.A., stood on the deck of the steamer St Paul, bound for New York, waving a little square of white handkerchief. His wife remained below. At the precise moment you slid with curled palms on to the cotton sheets of your mother's delivery bed, Prince Frederick Augustus of Saxony fell from his horse and sustained a slight fracture of the skull.'

I didn't laugh. How could I? It might be true. She has such a fertile imagination.

'Oh darling,' I said. 'Darling, what if it were true?'

'Well, it is,' she asserted. 'Oh yes, and here's a very strange thing. Someone far away in Bohemia or Moravia' (I'm quite sure she had been reading a book on the period) 'was writing a letter to the newspapers saying he was disturbed by the growing amount of anti-semitism. Now if that's not an omen, what is?'

I wrote it all down in my notebook in shorthand – what she'd told me. I felt quite unwell. Almost as if I'd been present at my own beginnings and if I'd only had the knowledge or the strength I could have cried out 'No, not now – later. Don't give birth to me now, it's not fair.' It isn't fair. I shouldn't have been born then. I still have it all in my notebook though I can't read my own writing. She seemed to know a lot more about when I was born than about when she was born. Except the text from the Bible on her day was 'And God saw everything he had made and behold it was good'. She wouldn't tell me what my text was. Maybe she genuinely didn't know, but it still worries me, not knowing and thinking that maybe she knows, and it might be much more enlightening than all that rubbish about the General with his handkerchief, and Augustus falling off his horse.

I asked Claude last night if Lily had ever told him about the day he was born, but he was too distracted, too depressed suddenly to concentrate on anything poor little me had to say. 'Have another drink,' he said, pouring out more of the dreadful stuff and encouraging me to sing again. He began to walk restlessly about the room and put on a record whose words I couldn't catch – except for something like 'Who's as blue as me, ba-a-by?' My head really was tormenting me: eyes smarting, heart swelling up and up like a brown paper bag – the agony before it splits. I turned my back on them all, hoping they would at least have the decency to notice I was suffering. I felt so light-headed. There's such a bundle of me always, nothing like the real me at all (though it's only to be expected that I should be all swollen and gorged after an operation such as I had) and I might almost be in disguise. I do wonder who those stubby little feet belong to, and what trick of the light makes my hair look like Flanders wire, and why my teeth have all rotted away, because inside I'm just as I always was – a trim little figure, not thin ever, but firm and shapely and such beautiful glossy hair, and such an air about me of gaiety and flirtatiousness and womanly warmth.

'What's up, Shebah?' asked Victorian Norman, from somewhere. Don't think I couldn't guess how his hand, hidden from view, was caressing the neck – such a ladylike column of a neck – of Julia. Maybe Claude knew it too.

'Don't you bloody well know?' I shouted, because I don't have to be polite to Norman. Friends we are. Friends! Lily did a painting last winter of the three of us sitting on the sofa, with the paraffin lamp dangling just above my head. Why she had to put that in I can't imagine, though there may be some symbolism. It was very clever, the painting, because though she couldn't have intended to capture it quite so subtly, we all looked so joined together by blobs of paint, so chummily bunched together, and yet on each of the three faces (though it doesn't look in the least like me – and why she had to paint those scarves round my head I don't know) there was such a look of distaste, such enmity in spite of the friendly grouping. And that's how we are really. I despise this so-called friendship, and I despise Victorian Norman and his disrespect, and I despise Lily for her so-called kindness, because she never stops picking my brains and taking the credit for it. They are all headed for disaster and they all approach it with such overwhelming *ennui* and lassitude. It hardly matters where I'm heading or in what frame of mind, seeing I was born in 1899 and have received nothing but blows on the head ever since. Claude came round the back of my chair and peered into my face. 'Go away,' I said, flapping at him with my handkerchief, sniffing and yet still smiling, though there was a little gust of irritation beginning to eddy upwards.

'Ah, my love,' he crooned, the lying swine, squatting at my feet. Behind us no doubt Norman and Julia were quite at liberty to do exactly as they wanted.

'An excess of secretion from the lachrymal gland flowing on to the cheek as tears,' said Claude, quite insane, while I dabbed at my poor weak eyes, and all the gay cheekiness evaporated slowly, and I felt so angry and so weary. I wanted to hit him. I don't utterly dislike Claude. He can be kind.

'You're all such fools,' I said. I can't remember exactly what I said, though I could have bitten my tongue in two afterwards, with regret. I must have said that Lily really thought him a bloody fool and that she only continued the friendship for all the outings it afforded her and the free drink, and a lot about Norman being after Julia and how Lily was encouraging him. And after all that, after speaking so indiscreetly and with such malice, though it was the truth, he said so calmly, still sitting at my feet with his fingers playing with his beard, 'Very probably, Shebah, very probably.' I can't help myself, I don't want to be disloyal, though God knows they all crucify me ten times a day, but I get so irritated and my words are only a form of vomit. I have no control and no ease till the last little morsel of half-digested hatred is spat into their faces. I sat feeling dreadfully weak then and ashamed. Suddenly two tears welled up in Claude's eyes and spilled, without breaking, on to his shirt. I could have died. I couldn't tell him it was excess secretion from his lachrymal gland or whatever, and I couldn't erase what I had said, but fortunately nothing followed the two tears. His eyes dried up, and behind us there were scuffling noises and the voice on the record stopped asking 'Who's as blue as me, ba-a-by?' though I might have told him.

'Get up, Shebah,' Claude said, 'come and look out of the window and smell the air.' He pulled me up out of the chair quite gently, though for all I know it might have been then, in that singular moment, that he decided to shoot me when he got the opportunity. Norman and Julia were no longer in the room. I was quite startled. He didn't seem to notice – just took hold of my hand and drew me to the window and began clearing the objects from the sill and putting them on the gramophone lid: a little white figure with a parasol and a large silver tea pot and an orange candlestick with a small stuffed bird sitting within its centre cup. The little bird rolled on to the floor when he moved the candlestick and I picked it up for him – such a soft-textured creature with glass eyes sewn into the down on either side of its pointed beak. We leaned together on the wide sill overlooking the little yard and the garden beyond. 'Aaah,' I said, taking only little snapping gulps and wishing I could unsay all I had said a moment ago. 'Aaaah,' he breathed, inhaling the cold air and swelling his huge chest. The light from the room shone right on to a tree below and made its leaves so green, so lovely. The wistaria curled over the sill we leaned on, and Claude played with its leaves as if they were an extension of his beard. I was worried about Norman and Julia. I hoped they weren't out there in the grass beyond the light. I didn't want Claude to be made more unhappy, though maybe I don't understand any of them. I asked Claude about Lily, tentatively this time. I really didn't want to do any more harm. 'Do you think she loves Edward?' I said, and it was difficult for me, because I had spoken so slightingly about love.

'Not yet,' he said, and turned to look at me, half his face in shadow, and one eye in utter darkness. 'There will,' he continued, and God knows what he meant, and probably it was all words, 'be a worse agony yet to come.'

'But why, darling, why?'

'I can't tell you, Shebah. I only know it to be true. Lily will fall, and Billie will be as nothing.'

'Oh yes, darling,' I said, 'that was dreadful. Poor darling Lily.' And I meant it. I do mean it. She *was* unhappy – so excited about Billie coming home and so hopeful for the future and we all stayed away deliberately, and then I met Norman in the street and he said, 'Haven't you heard? Lily is very ill, and Billie is gone.' Of course I don't know what happened, even now, but I did hear she tried to kill herself. It's hard to be certain about Lily. It's so short a time ago, and yet here she is seemingly none the worse for it and with another devoted lover already breathing her name as if she were a goddess. Nothing seems to check her or break her growth. Any setbacks only serve to accelerate her progress.

'Yes, dreadful,' said Claude.

I did feel it was real for a moment. Of course sitting here now with them all sprawled out on the grass it doesn't seem dreadful at all. They're so resilient. But the air last night, so chill, so cool, and the quiet room so filled with treasures, and the wine inside me and my guilt, and the memory of those two realistic, unchangeable tears that had spilled so terribly from Claude's eyes, made everything seem truly without hope. And I almost – yes, almost – felt I'd crossed the gulf that separated them from me, because for once I hadn't merely shared and sympathised with their general suffering but had in some way contributed to it. It did occur to me then that it was this factor, this tangling and goading that went on between them, that united them so strongly. They are all partial fashioners of each other's despair, a touch here, a deceit there, words spoken out of turn, hypocrisies, insincerities, insanities binding them like glue and making them in the end indestructible.

I was so busy last night thinking these thoughts, which are all so much damn rubbish, and worrying my head for answers, that I didn't realise Claude too had left the room. Without him at the window it was just another window and I felt cold, so I put all the things back on the ledge and the little brown bird, which reminded me of a song, and I hummed the tune and felt quite clear-headed.

> All through the night there's a little brown bird singing,
> Singing in the hush of the darkness and the dew . . .

Propped against the wall was a painting of a nude woman with long hair, and a little dog snuffling in her lap. A very golden painting, though my eyes are half useless. I had to bend down to look at it closely and I half fell over, which made me laugh, and there I was sprawled on the carpet laughing and one of the dogs woke up and pushed its nose into my chest. Really very like the painting. Though the days when I loll about without my clothes are long since past. Not that they ever began. I didn't want Claude to think there was an atmosphere, so I began to sing 'Let's Start All Over Again'. I felt the more noise I made and the more gaiety there seemed to be distilled, the quicker the sadness would evaporate. And I didn't want anyone to think I was listening to conversations, though everything was very still, and I didn't care to think what Victorian Norman was about.

I kept remembering something Lily had said about Miss Evans, the hair-remover – how she'd gone into her son's room and found a used 'conservative' on the mantelpiece. At the time they all laughed themselves silly over it and I thought they were mad, but I can see now that it's somewhat humorous, though perhaps with spending so much time together, I mean a whole weekend like this, I'm becoming as obsessed as the rest of them. Not that I know for sure what those things look like, though in that house when Eichmann Hanna was bringing his women in every night there were some disgusting things thrown down the toilet. The extremes there are in living. Flushing the toilet in that evil-smelling little cubicle and through the broken pane of glass, one star, six-pointed and diamond-white, a million light years away, still giving forth such a pure and crystal memory above my weary head.

I got up off the floor and peeped out of the window into Claude's garden, but I couldn't see anything but a multitude of leaves, and while I was looking Claude himself came back into the room, as noiselessly as he had left. I did feel better, more naturally gay, and he looked gayer too, more calm, and his eyes though still half barbarous, smiled at me. He is a barbarous man despite his preoccupation with glass and china and everything fragile: a primitive man, half covered in hair, moving about the bejewelled room, humming softly, picking things up continually, searching with his hands among the pictures and the ornaments for yet more packets of cigarettes and more bottles of wine. Save for the absence of wings he looked like a great furred bee. There was still no sign of Julia and I thought I had better sing again to make things easier. At that moment, Lily, in a pink-striped nightgown, almost jumped into the room on top of me, with Norman behind her.

'Oh darling, darling,' I cried, because there was no sign of Edward, and Claude had talked about a worse agony to come, but she certainly didn't look agonised – in fact rather peaceful and rosy in that striped nightgown. You can never be sure though, for the lighting is so poor and my eyes are so weak, and she might have been upset. She told me that she just felt like a cigarette and wasn't tired and that he, Edward, was asleep. They just don't seem to need sleep. Not tired after a whole day of talking and travelling and drinking! And the emotional energy she must have expended during the last hour or so. I simply haven't had enough of that sort of experience to know where their energy comes from. Lily says it's because she re-charges herself through her emotional life. I just don't know. Every day I undergo a thousand emotional scenes and yet I never cease to have a feeling of weariness and inertia. Norman and she used to argue about it for hours until my head throbbed. She said it was the way in which energy was directed that determined whether one was refreshed or not. She said that energy was nothing but the instinctual power of sex, which could be sublimated into other useful activities like bathing a baby or painting a picture, but that sooner or later the sublimations would gradually lead to a mood of tiredness. Norman said it was all rubbish, that it was a question of the food we eat, the amount of protein in the diet. I do feel Norman could be right, though I despise him so, and he certainly has never bothered to sublimate himself, not for one day. Lily never used to express herself so clinically until that American came along with his terrible theories. I always knew I was an hysteric, that I had an unstable temperament, thank God, of which I was quite aware before she got hold of all those books on neuroses, but she did tell me that the word hysteria came from the Greek for uterus. It's all so fantastic, so unbelievable, so unpoetic. That little star that shone through the broken pane of glass in that rotting house was unbelievable too, but so pure, so grandly scientific and cosmic, but all this other business is so bound up with bowels and tumours and unpleasant things – and I ought to know, because when I had my operation they removed almost everything, including my hysteria too most likely. It did use to be different. There was another mode of living, of courtship; even if I myself have never experienced it, it does exist. People had houses and gave dances and hung little lanterns in trees, and fragrance billowed outwards when the waltzing began. Lily could never compete in such circumstances. She admits the possibility of a relationship with a man would cause her acute embarrassment if she couldn't interpret it physically. She never walks anywhere. Apart from going up and down the escalators in Lewis's she never takes any exercise. To be fair, there was a time when she and Norman, after midnight, would run twice round the Cathedral, but that was nothing but eccentricity.

Ah, the walking I did. My feet were so tantalisingly small, my hair so satisfactorily thick, a great bunch of it hanging down my back. Walking along the promenade, a group of us chattering away, and always such heroic sunsets, and later, a single star coming out and the wind beginning to blow more strongly as I craned my head backwards and stared upwards out of weak eyes. Then suddenly, like a firework display, the whole sky would be encrusted with planets and globes and stars, and the moon, perfectly round, would rise above the black, oily river. I won't say it was all beautiful. Some of my so-called friends were dreadful fools. Their banality robbed my heart of heights of happiness. There were times when I felt oppressed by a sense of omission, a feeling that I was utterly alone, that the words I mouthed continually were words behind glass and nobody could grasp their meaning – at least not the fools I knew. They made me feel weary all right. Some time I must ask somebody who knows about these things. I never fail to be surprised when I read that great people, great artists, feel exactly as I do. But nobody I actually meet or attempt to communicate with ever feels a damn thing. Perhaps Lily does a little, when she's in a serious frame of mind – between men. While I was curious last night as to why she wasn't safely tucked up with Edward, I was really more anxious about her and Claude being together. All those deplorable things I had told him. And he really did seem a shade aloof with her. Oh, he smiled and gave her a cigarette and some more to drink, but he went over at once to talk to Norman and left her sitting alone in the armchair. Julia came out of the bedroom, though I can't remember her going in, and I tried to talk to her. I held her hand for a moment, and it was dry and burning. I said how much Lily admired Claude (I was lying) and how they understood one another so well.

'Yes, they do, Shebah,' – such a polite little voice, though it's only the way Julia shapes her vowels so beautifully – and I began to fear lest I was doing more damage. She is his mistress, and the relationship between Claude and Lily is rather strange, and maybe Julia is distrustful anyway. So I just gabbled on, audacious as ever, allowing my voice to become a little more contralto, thinking what the hell did it matter anyway, as in a very few hours I would be banished from this silver and china room and forgotten in my own hovel. Lily sat quite still with her eyes closed and a glass in her hand and a meaningless little smile curving her mouth. God knows what she was smiling at. Yet I did have a vague sorrowful emotion in my heart. If I have a heart. Other people of my age (no, I can't bear it) have hearts that split and wheeze and thunder, necessitating long weeks in bed and an enormous amount of attention. Tender mauve grapes arrive hourly and are placed in colourful heaps on the bedside table. Bunches of daffodils, invalid yellow, are stuck in vases on the window ledges. I can't stand the anguish of being without an ailing heart. That that too should be denied me! One day without preliminaries the beating will just stop, the blood stop flowing. No one will guess, let alone enquire. I shall lie frozen for ten days without a heartbeat in an empty house. The forlornness of it!

I half expected Edward to run in and pick up Lily without a word and carry her away, and I told Julia as much, but she said she thought he was probably fast asleep, as if she knew out of her own experience that this would be the case. Such a nice girl and very well mannered. We talked about the theatre and about her job before she met Claude, and about Claude's improved health – mental, that is – though as far as I can see he's still raving, and about the dogs and the names of all the animals' relations and how when they are in pup you leave them quite alone (I'd leave them alone at all times) and about Lily. Not very much about Lily – only she did let slip that Billie had actually come here one Sunday when Lily was staying for a couple of days. It was only a matter of weeks ago, and Lily and he had gone into another room to discuss things.

'What things, darling?' I said.

But she was evasive, perhaps she really didn't know, and then she made the observation that Billie appeared to be charming but evidently wasn't. I didn't tell her what I thought of Billie, the rotten swine, talking to me as if I was nobody, always glad to see the back of me, when I had more right, more need to be there, than he had. Grudging me a couple of hours in a damp eroded kitchen. I hadn't a large flat to return to, or two devoted parents, or friends and relations sending parcels once a month regularly as clockwork, with home-made plum cake and tins of tobacco, a new pair of socks – just as if he hadn't a large enough salary to buy his own. Why is it that those in receipt of more than their fair share of the vanities of life can't bear the very poor even a tiny allotment of comfort? When he went away and I used to stay sometimes at Lily's overnight, in that vast sinful brass bed, with all those poor stuffed animals staring with pebble eyes from each corner of the room, and Victorian Norman banging up and down stairs all night, I used to get such pleasure from thrusting my fist backwards through the head bars of the bed and knocking the photograph of Billie from its nail on the wall. Lily would mutter from the sofa under the mound of duffel coats and curtains that served her as bedding, 'What's up, Shebah?' and I would reply, 'Oh God, I don't know, the whole place is like Grand Central Station,' and think of Billie face downwards with his well-shaped nose full of dust, under the bed on which so many nights he must have lain supreme. I didn't really want to stay overnight at Lily's. There were so many things I ought to have done, my bit of fish to be placed in salted water, my body to attend to, my eye drops, but it was all too much to cope with, and it was always so cold, or snowing or blowing a gale, and Lily would say so enticingly, with such warmth, 'No, Shebah, dear Shebah, do stay. You can't go back there.' And of course latterly it was just impossible to return there, even to think about it. The house was empty, and Eichmann Hanna had been removed by the authorities and everything was falling apart and the gas was cut off and the electricity cut off, and the dust and the dirt blew heedlessly up and down the stairs. There was water pouring through the roof and snow beginning to pile up in the hall. I ask you, what human being could live like that – persecuted by day and by night by all the alarms of a battlefield? They just wouldn't believe me when I told them what it was like. And then one night Norman walked me home and I couldn't open the door, and finally when we did enter and Norman shone his torch, there was sheet ice from vestibule to roof, a stairway of glass, and icicles hanging in petrified ribbons from the rotting banisters. Norman made a little noise, an intake of air, almost a sound of admiration. He stood playing his torch on the whole glacial scene. 'The mind boggles,' he said at last, and took me back to Lily. After that they were kind to me and I did stay for a longish time, but gradually there was a new dimension – or rather an old familiar dimension – of impatience, and then sly hints, and then they began to talk about Rooms to Let in front of me, so that I went out one morning and knocked at the first door that took my demented fancy and rented a room for the following Monday. I did think that their humanity would have made them pause and see how impossible it was for me to go on alone, but then Lily was leaving and Norman was going to take over the ground floor, and no one mentioned the idea of me living in Norman's old room, and how could I ask them? How could I, choking as

I was? So I just moved into another little hovel and left all my books and my records and my bits and pieces to rot in that refrigerator along the road. Of course it did thaw out eventually, but I hadn't the heart to go back and see all my belongings stained and obliterated and *his* inscriptions in my books washed out by nature's superhuman tears. Once I had gone from Lily's, removed so to speak from the necessity of having my suffering smelling to heaven right under their noses, they were good to me again. My appointments continued as before, and since Lily was recovering from the traumatic experience of Billie's return and sudden departure, we weren't disturbed. There was a difference of course. She seemed very withdrawn and would tell me nothing, absolutely nothing, about why she'd been ill and what had occurred. I had thought she was staying with her mother, and then one night I called round to ask Norman if there was any news and there was Lily passing down the hall, all skin and bone and eyes glittering and a mouth closed in a tight line as if she never intended to speak again. I was so taken aback I said, 'Oh darling, I had no idea, just pretend I'm not here,' and she walked on down the hall and shut the door behind her. I found myself hovering like a moth in the dim hall, not knowing what to do. Norman was no help, he was going out somewhere or other and no, he couldn't talk and no, I shouldn't stay, and yes, Lily was best left alone, till he almost forced me out of the house into the street and walked off whistling towards the bus stop. A few days later she did send me a little note asking me to call, and though she wasn't her old self (like now) she was grateful for my company. Of course I was hurt she wouldn't, couldn't, take me into her confidence. It had something to do with sweets, though whether she was alluding to the Sweetness of Life or merely to Quality Street, I've never fathomed. I did so want to understand

decay. It was a relief when it ended, when she left on the train for her worse agony to come, as Claude would have it. It was a relief to think that finally my peace, my certitude, my Friday night had seeped away like water down a drain, leaving only debris behind. But then, after all, I found she hadn't abandoned me. Victorian Norman has taken up, like a ritual handed down by his fathers, the ceremony of my Friday night. It's kind or it's cruel. I can't decide.

I was just about to tell Julia last night about a play I had been in, when she said she ought to put the kettle on, though that was a lie because I never saw a bloody cup of tea till this morning. When I turned to look at Lily there was only Victorian Norman sitting in an armchair, legs crossed. No sign of Lily, no sign of Claude. Gone like the dear dead days beyond recall. There was no use asking Norman for an explanation, so we just looked across the carpet at each other, him in his armchair and me on the sofa, heads sunk on our respective breasts, eyeing each other if not with affection, at any rate with understanding. 'Ho, ho, my love,' he said insanely, wobbling his foot in its splendour of shiny leather. I wouldn't give him the satisfaction of a reply. He laughed and closed his eyes and leaned his head back. Not an unpleasant face really, taking it all in all: perhaps a slight reflection of everyday life, of present-day life. I could just see him pleading for an embrace, mouth gently pursed. Not from me, naturally, but from some cool, efficient girl like Julia. Where have the men gone, I wonder? The splendid army captains in their peaked caps with their reckless ways? Norman might have been the hero in some pre-war musical, with his foppish hair and his brows arching up like two wings and his well-kept hands folded delicately on his lap. Not that he's good-looking by any means. Pathetic, rather. Hardly more than a child.

Norman began to snore. With each reverberation his upper lip trembled. A fly landed on his forehead and he woke and sat up and asked me, 'Where's Julia, Shebah?'

'She's putting the kettle on, darling,' I answered, noting the little dab of spittle at the corner of his mouth. My eyes seemed to be seeing far more clearly than usual. The leg of the piano, the one nearest to me, was shaped like the calf of a ballet dancer. Footless, it pirouetted and bulged with muscle.

'What's up, old girl?' Norman said.

Inconceivable he should be talking to me. *Old girl of mine*, he might have sung, *old pal of mine, I'm weary and lonely, it's true*. Before I could reply he stood and stretched himself and went downstairs. Like a stage direction for *A Midsummer Night's Dream*, Edward entered the room in pyjamas, the hem of his dressing-gown dragging across the carpet. Where do they get all this clothing from, I wonder? He looked out of the window and then went into the bathroom. I heard water gurgling into the basin. When he came out he was smoking a cigarette. He flicked a little mound of ash tidily into the hearth and went to stand at the window. He cleared his throat.

'Do you know where Lily is?' he asked.

'God knows,' I cried. 'Leaping from bed to bed, no doubt.' I hadn't really expected to say that – the words just shot out.

'A lovely night,' he said, after a moment. He had his back to me.

'Yes, dear, a lovely night for some,' I said.

Such children in their observations, their ability to be articulate about the obvious. I felt overdressed not being in night attire. The door downstairs opened. The alarm bell shattered the room. With a faint hum of irritation the fly rose in the air and spun under the ceiling. With a sense of purpose, God bless him,

Edward went to the head of the stairs and stood with folded arms. A sob, or perhaps a laugh, from half-way down, and then Lily with chilled shoulders and remote face appeared like an apparition. Edward went into the guest-room and Lily followed. Pretend I'm not here, I might have said. There was no need, she wasn't aware of me. The most disheartening thing about all this coming and going and change your partners and weekends in the country, is that there's no one, no one at all, to whom I can unfold this tale in all its magnitude. I simply wouldn't be believed. Or comprehended. It would be casting pearls before swine. I suppose I might drop to my friend, Mrs Malvolio, that I spent the weekend in an antique shop – the marvels hanging on the walls, the dear blue china plates rolling round the shelves. The praying angel would be appreciated. But can I possibly repeat that most of the guests spent half the night wandering about in night attire, that the host let fall two oval tears upon his checked shirt? Not to mention that before the night ended a hundred pounds of damage had been done, and that at dawn a bullet, whining like a bee, sped to my palpitating flesh.

No sooner had Lily and Edward removed themselves than Claude arrived half-way up the stairs, unclothed it seemed. The bare breasts came into view, nipples like raisins embedded in the white flesh.

'Claude, darling,' I screamed, not that I truly cared whether the whole damn lot of them ran round stark naked.

'It's all right, my love, I have my lower garments.'

He had been attending to his roses outside, he explained. Julia and Norman (where had they been?) lay down behind the sofa and began to pluck at a harp that lay on its side. I did think foolishly that she was waiting for the kettle to boil, otherwise I should have gone to bed. I can't allow myself to dwell on what happened later. Those little broken figures and the pieces of glass lying on the carpet. It was an accident. I'm not usually accident-prone, or predisposed to being clumsy. With what shame and remorse, with burning face and throbbing head, I retired to bed.

'Good night, darlings. Oh, darling.'

'Good night, my love.'

'Good night, Shebah.'

'Sleep well, my dove.'

I didn't really sleep. I was too confused. This morning, at least before my accident (as it's been described), Claude was very kind, very generous. Without suspicion, trustingly, I rose and cleaned my face and went out into the garden among the roses and the trees. Edward's head wavered between two branches and a cloud of leaves. A bird sang and the sun shone palely overhead. When I was shot I distinctly heard Victorian Norman laughing. God forgive him.

It's been quite an interesting two days. I feel a little guilty that I didn't talk more to Edward. I seem to remember Lily telling me that I should say nice things about her to him. I imagine Claude said enough nice things for all of us. Nobody said anything nice about me, and I was fired upon at close range. Not such a surprising occasion after all. Have I not been reviled, cursed, wounded, all my life? Did not Prince Augustus of Saxony sustain a fracture of the skull the moment I was born?

The monotony of it all. While they lie indolent in the sun, assured of their worse agonies to come, I wait with closed eyes. For something, someone . . . for two great and gentle hands to lift me from my cross . . . for anything . . .

7

'We must go,' the man said again. He sounded angry and a little unhappy.

His wife put down the photograph at once and rose to her feet, smoothing her skirt down with her hands. 'All right,' she said, 'What time is it?'

'Gone one, and I've a meeting at three.' He turned in a businesslike way to Claude and held out his hand. 'It's been very pleasant meeting you, Mr Perkins. May I ask if I hire a van to fetch my desk, or do you manage that side of it?' He made to disengage his hand, but Claude held it firmly.

'As a general rule I let my customers make their own arrangements,' said Claude, 'but you live quite near, so I'll deliver it personally. Some time next week – maybe Monday or Tuesday. Tuesday most like, man.'

'That's very good of you. Much obliged.'

'Do come again some time,' invited Julia vaguely.

The couple got into their car. It was a big shiny car and there was a fluffy toy dangling from a string in the rear window. The woman didn't wave goodbye. She bent her head, as if looking for something, and then the car drove off up the street.

Julia went straight into the kitchen and began to attend to the child's nappies. Claude squatted beside the sink and put his hand in the waste bucket. 'That fellow's cheque is in here somewhere,' he said.

'His cheque?'

'You swept it up, my love. It's there somewhere. Look for it, Ju, when you've a moment.'

He stood upright and went out into the yard. He wiped his fingers on the white pillow in the pram. He decided he would deliver the desk in two weeks' time, not one. He would put his arm about the woman and get her to confide in him. They would become friends and he would make her life richer, more varied. He would help her to sort out her husband.

Entering the barn, he walked its length until he came to the green sofa. He often sat here when he wanted to be alone. No one could spy on him, because it was impossible to see through the little window: the glass was too dim, and the creeper that climbed about the barn was too thick. He sat down and took the letter from his pocket and read it.

Sunday, September 4th, 1960

Dear Flower,

Could you send me that photograph you took of us in the garden. It's urgent. I don't think Edward wants to marry me after all. Actually, it doesn't really matter because I'm not pregnant now. I must have got my dates muddled. Anyway, I don't think Edward likes me very much – I can sort of tell. I don't particularly want to marry him, but I would like a chance to refuse, if you know what I mean. How are you and Julia? Norman says he tried in the barn but Julia wasn't having any. I want the photo just to show Edward. If it's a pretty one, I mean if I look quite nice, maybe he'll like me again. Please don't forget. Norman says Shebah wore her bandage for weeks, till it fell off with filth. Are you happy? If Edward does vanish I shall just live a normal, sensible life – no more messes or intrigues. This time I mean it. Don't laugh. Have you read a man called Wallace Stevens?

> *There is or may be a time of Innocence,*
> *There is never a place. Or if there is no time*
> *If it is not a thing of time, nor of place –*

and something and something. There's a lot more like that. He used to go up and down in lifts in America. He worked in Insurance. Please take care. You could light a candle for me. Blessings, L.

P.S. I'm a bit anxious really. I know I'm not pregnant by Billie, but I may well be by Edward. Isn't it awful!

Claude read the lines of verse several times without making much sense of them. He decided Lily had probably remembered them wrongly or disordered the punctuation. He folded the letter neatly and rose from his seat and went to the newly bought desk. Opening the right-hand drawer he thrust the letter into the darkness for the woman to find and read. He returned to the house and climbed the stairs to the living-room. He picked up the photograph from off the sofa and propped it on the mantelpiece. Through the window he noticed the cat from next door moving across the yard to lose itself in the long grass of the little garden. Sucking strands of beard in at the crinkled corner of his mouth, he went downstairs.

The photograph remained on the mantelpiece for a long time. It accumulated dust and was bent at one corner. On the right-hand side there were three figures, two of them sitting on the ground and the third slumped scowling on a wrought-iron bench, skirt stretched tight over stout thighs. On the left, isolated, hunched, crouched the fourth figure, not looking into the camera. The sun had gone behind a cloud.

The three friends posed on, marooned in a summer garden.